COMING OUT

leroy

sylvia aguilar-zéleny

E

EPIC
Press

Leroy
Coming Out: Book #3

Written by Sylvia Aguilar-Zéleny

Copyright © 2016 by Abdo Consulting Group, Inc.

Published by EPIC Press™
PO Box 398166
Minneapolis, MN 55439

Printed in the United States of America.

Cover design by Nicole Ramsay
Images for cover art obtained from Shutterstock.com
Edited by Nancy Cortelyou

LIBRARY OF CONGRESS CATALOGING-IN-PUBLICATION DATA

Aguilar-Zéleny, Sylvia.
Leroy / Sylvia Aguilar-Zéleny.
p. cm. — (Coming out)
Summary: Seventeen-year-old Leroy is far from being happy, he is gay and doesn't
dare come out and disrupt his family. Leroy goes on an incredible yet painful and
terrifying journey from Dallas to Taos, and from fear to love.
ISBN 978-1-68076-009-5 (hardcover)
1. Homosexuality—Fiction. 2. Gays—Fiction. 3. Gay teenagers—Fiction.
4. Coming out (Sexual orientation)—Fiction. 5. Young adult fiction. I. Title.
[Fic]—dc23
2015932731

EPIC
Press

EPICPRESS.COM

To the three men of my life, Carlos, Juan and Ernesto. Thank you for your love and support.

CHAPTER ONE
leroy

NO ONE WOULD THINK I'M GAY. NOT ME. I'M the quiet dude in the class. I'm the smart one who only gets A's. I dress in neutral colors. I have a girlfriend. I have a gorgeous girlfriend. I don't have too many friends, but no one seems to care because, hey, I am the serious, nerdy student who is into art. No, no one would think I'm gay.

But I am.

I don't know if I was always gay though. There was a time when I liked girls. No, there was a time when I *thought* I liked girls. Tonya, for example. Yes, the first girl I liked was Tonya.

Tonya had big gray eyes, which made a beautiful

contrast with her black, almost purple skin. Tonya and her pink, fleshy lips. Tonya and her long, braided hair. Tonya and her multicolored fingernails. Tonya would always wear shorts, the kind that were once your favorite pair of jeans but your mama made into shorts because you grew taller. Tonya was tall, taller than me and taller than anyone else in class. Perhaps it was precisely because she was so tall that no one talked to her, or maybe because she didn't have real parents; she had a foster family. A white foster family.

I liked Tonya. I did. I wanted us to be friends; I wanted her to be my girlfriend even though we were in fourth grade. I wanted us to walk holding hands. I wanted us to ignore people's laughter because she was so tall and I was so, so, short. I wanted, oh, I wanted to take her home and tell Mama, "Look Mama, this is Tonya, she is my girlfriend." Mama would be so happy, and never ever would she call me little girl for crying over Oprah's guests, or singing Destiny's Child, or Beyoncé's songs. Yeah, I was *that* kind of boy.

I liked Tonya so much because she didn't look like other girls. She was more like a boy. The only girlie thing about her was the long hair. She was rough. She was strong. She was *different* too.

But I had no future with Tonya, or any other girl as I later learned. Because the one day I gathered the courage to go and tell her, "Hey, Tonya, wanna be friends?" Tonya looked at me, as if my words had been the most disgusting thing she ever heard. "Friends? I am not friends with boys like *you*," she said. I was such an idiot.

I should have left, it was clear she despised me, but instead I said, "Come on, why not? We can walk to school together, we can do homework, we live so, so, close. We can also . . . " Tonya stopped me in my tracks, and said "I ain't gonna be friends with no sissy-boy like you."

An idiot, I tell you, I was an idiot.

That's how everyone started liking Tonya, because she called me sissy in front of everyone. She said the one word that no one had dared to use when talking about me. Everyone started liking Tonya because she had crushed me like a spider on the sidewalk.

By the end of the school year I stopped being Leroy, and became Sissy.

I had always been well aware that I was *different*, I was well aware that everyone found me different, not because I was too short, or too shy, or too useless in sports. They found me different because they said I acted, I moved, and behaved like a girl. Can't blame them, I hated myself for that, too. For being a sissy.

No one likes a sissy. No one chooses a sissy for their team. No one plays with the school's sissy at recess. Being a sissy is shameful, sinful. No, I didn't wanna be a sissy, or maybe it was more that I didn't want people to think I was one. I wanted to be like everyone else. I wanted to be the boy everyone wanted to hang out with, the one they chose for the team, the one everyone would want for president of their class.

I promised myself that fifth grade was going

to be different. So I spent the summer watching Kendell, my brother, playing ball with his friends and hanging out with them down the street. I told myself, "If I start being more like *that*, people will like me." I made him my model. I started paying more attention to the way Kendell moved, acted, talked, breathed.

Kendell is four years older than me, so we shared nothing except a room. He had his own friends, his own hobbies, and he didn't want me around. He would push me around and kick me out of our room if he felt like it. He would curse and call me names. He would take the remote out of my hands to watch whatever he wanted on TV.

So, one day I went and asked him to teach me about sports, movies, and girls.

Kendell said, "You don't learn about all this shit, dork, you just know about it. Sports, girls . . . you? Why?"

I could have lied, but instead I said, "'Cause I don't want to be called sissy no more."

"Who called you sissy?" Kendell asked punching his fist into the other palm. I imagined him punching the shit, as he would say, out of whoever dared to call me sissy.

"Everyone," I said.

"Who's everyone?"

"Everyone in my class. Everyone in school. Everyone, just everyone. And I hate it." I started crying. Kendell didn't know what to do. He started patting my back, saying, "Don't cry, don't cry, Leroy, don't cry or you'll actually be acting like a sissy."

"Don't call me sissy, asshole."

"See, that's more like it. You ain't sounding like a sissy now," he said.

"I want everything to be different."

Kendell looked disappointed that he could not kick the shit out of all the kids at Jefferson Elementary School. He remained silent for a moment, then said, "We'll show 'em you're a badass."

Kendell and I became closer. For the first time, he started lending me his precious comics. He would invite me out with his friends to hang out or bike. "Come on, let's go talk shit with the guys," he said.

He also started teaching me how to fix this or that around the house. I hated it, and I sucked at it, but I kept on it. I changed from Oprah to MTV to be around my brother all the time. I became an obedient apprentice. We would have long movie marathons with men fighting, shooting, getting drunk, getting high, or speeding in cars, movies I really didn't care about, but movies I needed to learn from. I know by memory all *The Fast and the Furious* series, I swear.

For the rest of that summer, every day, before Mama came home from school, we would shoot some hoops, practice some punches, whatever Kendell thought would kick the sissy out of me.

"A sissy is soft," Kendell would say, "So don't be soft. Spit, curse, do whatever the hell you want. Scratch your balls, check out women's boobs, be a man. We can kick the sissy out of you."

But I don't think we kicked the sissy out of me. If anything, I learned to hide it. My manhood was shaped. It deceived people. With enough practice, nobody would ever know who I really was.

The next time Tonya tried to call me sissy, she didn't see it coming. I went from loving her to hitting her right in her face. It all started when our P.E. teacher left us on the court taking shots. I missed one, and she made fun of me.

"Shut up," I told her. I missed another and she did it again, she called me a sissy. I walked right up to her and punched her in the nose. "Don't you ever call me sissy. Don't you ever," I told her.

Tonya was hurt, her big gray eyes started tearing, her nose bleeding.

"What happened here?" our P.E. teacher asked when she got back on the court.

I balled my fists, and told Tonya with a stare not to open her mouth.

"Nothing, the ball, I didn't see it," she said.

Tonya was sent to the nurse. Right then and right there, in front of every one of my classmates, I grew like five feet taller.

Soon, word was out: "Leroy is a sissy no more." Everybody started looking at me as if I was that character from the David and Goliath story. I even drew an image of me punching Tonya in my scrapbook.

Yes, I was *that* David. I turned into him. I was not the school's sissy anymore. Correction, I wasn't *called* the school's sissy anymore. The truth is I never stopped *being* one, I just worked hard so that no one would know it. And I must have done the greatest job at it, because no one messed with me again at Jefferson. Even Mama, Mama stopped saying I acted like a little girl, too.

She was proud—proud of her two boys. Until she stopped being proud of Kendell because of all the shit he got himself into. Then I became her favorite, her smart little man.

Before the school year was over, Tonya left because she was sent to live with a new foster family. A black one, or so she told the class when our teacher told her to take this chance to say goodbye. My Goliath was gone.

Part of me felt that maybe, without her around, I could now stop trying so hard to be a man, I could stop trying to prove what a badass I was. I could bring back what I had learned to hide, the real me. But part of me knew that there would be other Tonyas, there would always be kids ready to make fun of me because they found me too *different* from them. The lie had to continue, the lie had to become a part of my life. I had to make believe that I was just like any other boy at school, even though I knew I wasn't.

I've been lying ever since.

Lying is like a chain, a chain you carry around, a heavy chain you have to live with because you don't want to be hurt. But the chain hurts. It hurts because you can't move freely; you can't be free. My chain keeps the sissy inside, keeps it in place. But I live a double life. I'm just like any other guy at school, but when I'm not in school, when I'm not at home, when I'm not anywhere near where people know who I am, I am me. I am a gay guy looking to score. And yes, I end up scoring with other guys like me, afraid of the truth. Afraid of *their* truth. Sissies who, just like me, lie every single day. The question is, how long will I be chained to this lie? How long can I restrain myself from acting as gay as I really am?

* * *

"Hey."

"Hey, yourself."

Sharon kisses my nose and then my lips.

"Are you daydreaming again?" she asks as she rests her arms on my shoulders.

"No, I'm not."

"You sure? I've been watching you sitting here looking at the sky for the last seven minutes."

"Seven minutes?"

"Yes."

"You were timing me and everything?"

"Yup."

"And how come you didn't wake me up?"

"Because you looked SO handsome," she says. "What was on your mind, another girl?" It's funny that Sharon is right; another girl *was* on my mind. Tonya and my sissy days were on my mind.

Sharon is my girlfriend. Yes, my girlfriend. Yes, *I* have a girlfriend. We've been together for almost six months now. She has everything you want in a girl, great looks, amazing body, sense of humor . . . If she had a dick she would be perfect.

We met in art class. She used to praise my drawings. We started talking. She's a great painter herself, and a great writer, she just doesn't give a shit about art all that much. Or at least she pretends not to. She wants to fit in with her group of friends, and to fit in she has to pretend she doesn't give a shit about anything but clothes, shoes, and boys.

Anyways, we started hanging out. It was clear since the beginning that she liked me; it would have been very stupid of me not to take advantage of that. I know that makes me look like an ass. But I liked her too. I did, just not in the same way. I do like hanging out with her, when she's not around her friends. She is someone you can talk to, she listens, she really listens. She could become an amazing playwright. She's in charge of this year's play. She's adapting some short story by Toni Morrison.

I walk her home every day, and today I waited for her until after she met with her friends from Drama Club.

I kiss her and say, "Ready to leave?"

"Yup."

We walk next to each other, arm in arm.

"So, how was the Drama Club meeting?" I ask.

"It was okay. We're going to start rehearsing next week." Sharon then grabs my hand, clears her throat, and says, "Hey, are we still on for tonight?"

"Tonight?"

Sharon really loves me, so much that she believes she's ready. She told me so a couple of weeks ago. And now, now she has a plan.

"Yes, tonight. My parents left this morning, re-member?"

"And?"

"Where's your mind today? My parents left, Leroy; that means we can do *stuff*." Sharon stops cold, then stands in front of me giving me that look, as if she is saying, "Take me." She gets closer to me and kisses my neck. I decide to play stupid.

"Stuff? What do you mean?"

Sharon laughs and then whispers in my ear, "I mean sex, babe, sex." She softly bites my ear.

What am I going to do?

Then I remember I actually have a way out of this. "I forgot about tonight and Mama wants to have a family meeting. Didn't I tell you about it this morning?"

"Are you serious?"

"Yeah."

"Is this about your brother again?"

"I don't know."

"Well, my parents won't come back until to-morrow night, so maybe you can spend Saturday morning with me. Think about it."

I have nothing to think about, there's no way I'm having sex with her. I mean, why would I? Would it even work?

Before I know it, we are outside Sharon's. I kiss her goodbye, a soft kiss barely touching her lips. She pulls me, she kisses me. I can feel her tongue knocking on my lips, wanting to come in. I follow her lead, but I can't help feeling uncomfortable. She tries to convince me to stay with her at least for a little while. I tell her I can't. She doesn't look mad, but she isn't happy either.

"You know you want it as much as I do," she says.

I say nothing. She kisses me again. "Call me or text me later, okay?" she asks. I nod.

Oh, Sharon. She wants me to be her first time. She believes she will be my first. She believes I am a virgin. But I'm not. Or maybe I am, 'cause I've never had sex with a girl.

Yes, I have had sex. Just not with girls.

My first sex encounter left me confused. I had just turned fifteen. It's not that I didn't like it; I wasn't sure what I was doing. He was older than me, like twenty or twenty-one, and he knew what he was doing.

It happened in a bathroom at the Galleria Dallas mall.

"I heard they caught two men doing it at the mall," said Lucy, one of my classmates. We were talking about sex. Well, no, actually my friends were talking about sex, I was just listening. Now that I think about it, none of us questioned her words or felt curious to know whom she heard this from. "Imagine how embarrassing—getting caught not only having sex, but having sex with a man," she ended.

The image of two boys having sex nearly gave me a hard on. That story, and the threat of being caught, didn't discourage me or scare me at all. If there was some gay action going on, I wanted to be part of it.

The truth is, I hadn't been all that curious about sex. I knew I was *different*; I knew I was gay. I knew I didn't like girls, except for girls' stuff. I knew I didn't like boys' stuff, except for boys. But I really hadn't thought of sex. Yes, I jerked off once in a while, but there was nothing in it, no fantasies or anything, just the pleasure of rubbing off. The pleasure of feeling.

I started going to the mall every other day. "All my friends hang out there," I would tell Mom, and she believed me. I walked up and down the whole building like a zillion times, but nothing. I never saw any action going on, but I discovered a new pleasure: people watching. Men watching.

Men, they were all over the place. Young men, older men. Tall men, short men. Handsome men, strong men, skinny men. All of them were right in front of me. They were everywhere, in groups of three or four just hanging out, talking shit, or with their girlfriends and friends window shopping. I was sorta window shopping, too.

I spent weeks doing that, then went home to fantasize about them. I would imagine making out with them, the same way kids my age do everywhere.

Watching, that is all I did before I actually got myself into something.

I was in the bookstore, checking out the comics when he approached me.

"Hey."

"Hey."

"You like comics?"

"Yeah, my brother has a huge collection, but he won't let me get close to it."

"Who's your favorite?" he said.

"Batman, I guess," I said without really thinking. It was only then that I looked at him; he had a beautiful smile and his skin was the color of sand. After an awkward silence, I asked him back, "Who's yours?"

"Spiderman, of course. He's the shit."

I was intrigued. "How so?"

"He's the most human of them all, he makes

mistakes, throws tantrums, he's actually a loser in everything else. He's the shit. I'm tellin' you."

There was something about the way he looked at me, something that led me to think he was into me. I wasn't wrong. He continued telling me about Spiderman for who knows how long, then he touched me on the shoulder and handed me one of his favorite Spiderman stories. He rubbed my back and caressed my hair for the longest moment in the world as I went through the pages.

I suddenly realized what was happening. I got a hard on. I didn't know what to do—I wanted to run to the bathroom—I reached with my hand, trying to hide what was obvious happening in my body.

He smiled. "It's okay, you just need to go to the bathroom," he said with a soothing voice. "Want me to take you?"

I nodded.

I followed him, my eyes moving from the floor to our surroundings; I certainly didn't want anyone to see me. We went to the men's bathroom, the last one on the second floor of the mall. There was no one in there. He held my hand and walked me inside.

He closed the door and looked at me, smiling. "I'll bet you're a great kisser," he said, and before I could say anything, he pulled my face to his and started kissing me. No, I wasn't a great kisser, I wasn't even a half-good kisser, but that day I became one.

He started on my lips, then my neck, my ears. My jeans started to feel tighter and tighter. He unzipped them and kneeled down. What was he doing? He probably noticed I was nervous, so he caressed my thighs, he caressed me around my bellybutton and said, "It's okay, don't worry, I won't hurt you."

He didn't hurt me, what he did was pleasing, what he did was hot, wonderful.

I burst it all out in a few seconds. I felt so embarrassed.

"I'm sorry," I kept saying. He cleaned himself up and smiled, and kissed me softly on the lips. "You are so cute," he said before he left.

I never saw him again.

I kept going to the mall, I kept going to the comics section at the bookstore, I kept window shopping, I kept looking for the guy, but nothing. He was nowhere to be found.

But the memory of him still lives with me. The memory of him holding my dick, playing with it, comes to me when I am all alone and I touch myself. His face has disappeared as the time has passed by. I probably wouldn't recognize him now. The only thing left is his hands on my dick.

On my way home, Sharon starts texting me. Her texting soon becomes sexting. I only reply with an emoticon, you know, the one with the blushed face. What else can I do? I don't know how much longer I can play the "I want to respect you" card with her. At some point, I will have to give in. I know it sounds stupid, but I kinda want to be her first one, not that I wanna have sex with her, but Sharon is important to me. I prefer to be the one who takes this step with her and not some asshole from school who would just hurt her.

Just the thought of sex with her gives me chills. How do you do it? How do you kiss and touch a body that doesn't arouse you? How do you whisper loving words to a girl you see as a close friend?

"What are you doing with her, Leroy?" I ask myself all the time. Pretending. That's what I'm doing. I'm pretending that I'm just like any other guy at school. When I decided to stop being called a sissy, I had to stop behaving like one, and to do so, well, you need to flirt with girls, you need to show yourself as a guy who drools every time he sees some cleavage or a round butt. I'm pretending I like girls when I'm absolutely sure that what I really like is men. How I wish Kendell were here. He would help me fix this mess my life is turning into.

kendell

I always knew my brother Leroy was a faggot. I've known it since we were kids. Okay, maybe I shouldn't say faggot, and maybe I'm exaggerating here; when we were kids I was too young to understand that he was gay. I just knew he was not like me; he was different from me and all the other kids. But I didn't really understand what that meant. I just had to put up with it.

See, those words—faggot, gay—they were in my vocabulary, but it was more like things you say without knowing exactly what they mean. You just used them because everyone else in your neighborhood does.

Then, when I was in ninth grade, I had this friend, Raymond. He told us his father had left his mother for a man. We were all like, "What do you mean, dude?" He explained it to us, he told us his old man was in love with another man. We were all like, "What the fuck?"

I know it sounds unbelievable that a kid would actually tell this story to everyone, but if you had met Raymond you would understand. Ray was the kind of kid who craved attention. The story of his father was perfect for him to be the school's sensation. "How is that even possible?" I remember asking him. It was through Raymond that I learned what a homosexual is. Ray said, "Homosexuals are men who like men, and women who like women."

"Like?" I asked.

"More than that, actually. Homosexuals fall in love, they have sex with each other. Homosexual sex. My dad, for example, was having homosexual sex with a man and my mother caught him in the act."

I was in shock. Raymond, who at that moment was the school's expert, explained that homosexual men act like women and that homosexual women act like men. That's when I thought of my little brother, that dumbass. Yes, Leroy sounded like these homosexual people Raymond was telling us about. Mama was on him all the time for acting like a little girl. *Oh shit*, I thought.

* * *

I started keeping an eye on Leroy, what he did, what he said. I noticed that he liked watching *Gossip Girl* instead of *Battlestar Gallactica*. I noticed how he held his cookies and his glass of milk. I noticed how he liked looking at himself in the mirror; he was like Mama, who never left home without checking her lipstick one last time.

Some time after I learned about homos, Leroy told me he was being bullied in school and called names. I wasn't mistaken. I wasn't the only one thinking my little bro was a homo. Leroy was one of those. He was in danger of becoming like Raymond's dad. I decided to help him, to help him be a real man. I didn't wanna have a homo for brother, no sir. I already had to deal with the jokes from the kids that lived in our building, jokes about Leroy being such a baby because he didn't want to climb trees, play on the street, or play war games.

Educating Leroy into the manhood business wasn't hard; he was so willing to change. He worked his ass off to shake the girlie out of him. Mama, who was always behind him, noticed.

"Don't you notice something in your little brother?" she asked me.

"What?"

"I don't know, he's more . . . "

"A boy."

She was happy; she wouldn't admit it, but she was happy. She was happy her son wasn't watching Oprah no more or singing all day long into a hairbrush microphone. It gave her one less reason to think she was fucking up our lives. Oh, yeah, Mama is like that. Yup, Mrs. Birdie Davis is the kind of mother who blames herself for our mistakes. Every time something happens to us, every time we fuck up . . . Okay, wait, no, every time *I* fuck up she goes, "Why? Why? What did I do? Where did I go wrong with you, Ken?"

Anyway, what I didn't know and what Leroy didn't know then, was that you can't shake the sissy away. You just can't. You are who you are. You can grow, you can evolve, you can change your looks, you can behave differently, but you can't change yourself. You are who you are, that's a fact.

I learned that the first time I ended up in juvie, but it has taken me years to actually understand it. Worse than that, it has taken me years to accept that Leroy, my only brother, is gay. Nothing will change that. There's no medicine for that, not even a good blow by the hottest girl on your street.

I wish I had understood that, and many other simple facts about life when I was outside, when I was free. I would have actually been of some help. Behind these bars I am no help, to Leroy, to Mama, to our little sister, Amber. Man, I can't even help myself, not in here.

'Cause, lemme say this, being in juvenile

31

detention is one thing, but being in jail is very, very, different. Here everyone hurts you just by looking at you. Walking with your eyes down don't even help. In jail you are hated, hurt, beaten, or raped just because. Just because people got pain, and they wanna pass that shit along.

The last time Mama and Leroy visited me, she told me I deserved to be here for what I did. She said I deserve to be behind these bars. Then Leroy cut in and told her, "Mama, don't say that," and I could tell she regretted her words, even though they was right.

"I hope that your time here is teaching you a lesson; I hope you understand that you can't go stealing and dealing on the street. That's not how I raised my kids," she finally said.

Mama was right, I knew that much, but I didn't say a word. What was there for me to say? I looked at her and then I looked at Leroy, he seemed so lost. I am the one locked up in here, but my brother, he is as locked up as I am.

I wish he could fucking visit me without her, so we could talk, brother-to-brother, man-to-man. It's not like I know what to say exactly, but these last months have taught me that all we have is our family. I don't want him to suffer, I don't want him to do stupid shit like I did just 'cause he feels trapped. That'd be shitty.

Leroy deserves better.

CHAPTER TWO
leroy

WHEN I WAS A LITTLE KID, ALL I WANTED WAS A doll, but all I got were the balls, trucks, and action figures that had once belonged to Kendell. Believe me, none of them were any fun for me. I think that's what got me into coloring books. You know, those old forgotten coloring books on sale at Dollar General? That was the closest thing to getting something new. We were so broke back then.

Anyway, thanks to the coloring books, before I knew it, I got myself into drawing. I would spend hours and hours working at our kitchen table. I can't explain it. I fell in love with painting. I used to tell Mama, "Mama, I wanna be an artist."

She would smile and say, "You can be whatever you want as long as you work your ass off." It made me laugh every time she said that.

"You said ass," I would say.

She would add, "And if you repeat it, I will kick *your* ass."

Mama did her best to get me stuff to draw first, and later to paint. She encouraged me not to follow the normal rules of art, but to try out new things and to paint my emotions. She would never say, "Paint the sky," or, "Make a drawing of a park." She would say things like, "Draw happiness," or, "Draw about how it feels to have an older brother." When I started reading, she would bring me biographies of famous artists. I read about Henri Matisse, I read about Gustave Moreau, I read about Picasso. I read about Jacob Lawrence, I read about women such as Lee Krasner, Gwendolyn Knight, and my favorite, Georgia O'Keefe. All of them became my art teachers. Learning about their styles of painting taught me how to shape my own.

Years went by.

Mama finished college and started working here and there. Kendell and I were still home alone all the time, but things were good. We had a better apartment, a better TV, and better food. Mama would take us once in a while to the store and say, "Get one toy. You can take whatever you want from this aisle." It was an aisle with cars and action figures. Things I didn't care about. I still wanted a doll, but because I knew I couldn't get one, I would choose a sketchbook, or crayons.

Drawing was my way out. Out of what? Out of my mind, my mind that kept fighting with the fact that I was living a lie. Drawing kept me busy, but I still wanted a doll. The perfect doll.

Then, I finally got one, a real one.

I was eight and Leroy was twelve when Amber was born.

Amber became the doll of my dreams, a doll I got to feed, dress, and rock—a flesh-and-blood baby. The toys, the clothes, the little shoes—everything I had always dreamed of was right there in our apartment. Amber became the model of many of my drawings and paintings. I loved her from the time I knew she was in Mama's belly.

Kendell, he wasn't too happy when Mama told us she was expecting. One: because he knew it meant a change in our economy; it was one more mouth to feed, and even though Mama now had a job, she also had student loans to pay. And two: Kendell knew that people would be talking about our mother because she was pregnant again and no man was around. Kendell complained when she first told us about being pregnant. He even called her a whore. Mama slapped him, and told him to shut the fuck up or he would never see the end of it.

That's Mama's punch line. For example, if we broke a plate, she'd yell, "You better sweep the floor or you'll never see the end of it." If we spilled milk on the table, she'd say, "You clean that table or you'll never see the end of it." When I was a kid I wondered what it looked like, "the end of it." I have never actually seen it. I've seen her mad, you betcha, but never too mad to see the end of what she always threatens us with. Kendell has though, and I wonder if Mama wishes she hadn't showed it to him all the time; maybe he got so used to experiencing the end of it that he would always get in trouble. Kendell has been in and out of juvie twice. But now things are worse. He got himself locked up in jail.

Kendell, Amber, and I have different dads and none of them has been around long enough to help Mama raise us, pay the bills, or fix the dishwasher. Mama did all that on her own. I am sure this is why she is so tough with us; she wants to make good men out of us. Unlike the men who got her pregnant.

Kendell says that unlike his father, who he barely

remembers, and Amber's, who we don't even know, my dad did try to make it work. I don't remember much about him—he's an old picture about to fade. I sorta remember a mustache, big brown eyes, and these hairy arms carrying me around, but that's it. Kendell remembers him. It seems he was the kind of father any child would want. "He was funny, he was nice, and oh, he loved Mama, so much that he was willing to be my papa too," Kendell told me once.

"And what happened?"

"Mama kicked him out."

"Why?"

"I dunno, and don't you go asking questions or . . ."

"I will never see the end of it."

Mama is tough, and that's one of the reasons I don't dare to tell her about me, about who I really am. She would be as mad as she gets with Kendell every time he ends up in trouble.

Seriously, if I tell her I am gay I will never see the end of it.

* * *

As I arrive home, I see my nine-year old sister, Amber, setting the table. She sees me and yells, "Mama, Leroy is here!"

"Mmhh, smells good, what's Mama making?" I ask her.

"Roasted chicken."

"Really?"

Unbelievable, no Chinese take-out tonight. We always have Chinese take-out on Fridays.

"You finally arrived. What took you so long?" Mama comes out of the kitchen. She has a salad bowl in her hands and puts it on the table. "Amber, you forgot the forks."

"Sharon had a meeting and I waited for her."

"Oh, isn't that romantic?" Mama smiled. "Meanwhile we are starving here."

"I'm sorry, I guess I should've texted you," I say as I leave my backpack on one of the chairs and grab a roll from the table.

"Wash your hands first. You too, Amber." She goes back in the kitchen.

"Come on, Amba girl, let's wash our hands," I say and pull my sister by her arm. "Were you starving?" I ask her.

"Not really, we had a snack when we got home from school."

Mama is a great cook. She says she learned how to cook real food when she worked for this old lady in a diner. No one makes chicken or pot roast like her. Her chicken noodle soup cures everything. Who cares about the family meeting? All I want is to eat. The roast-chicken smell permeates our apartment.

After washing our hands, Amber and I sit down; Mama brings the food and joins us.

"So, what's the occasion?" I ask.

"Yeah, Mama, why?"

"I have wonderful news, news that deserves a celebration," she says as she piles chicken and a spoonful of mashed potatoes on our plates.

"What's the news?" Amber asks.

"Yeah, what's the news?" I ask. Part of me wants her to say, "Kendell will be released," but I know we ain't that lucky.

"I received this job offer, a wonderful job offer," Mama says. She pauses, then takes a sip of her iced tea before adding, "And I am really considering it."

"You'll leave school? No more Happy Times?" I ask while serving myself some salad.

"Will I have to leave Happy Times too?" Amber asks.

Mama looks at both of us. She takes one more sip of her iced tea. "Actually, we will all have to leave our schools, our apartment, and this city. This job is in New Mexico."

"You can't be serious," I say, speaking with food in my mouth.

"New Mexico?" Amber asks.

"It's next to Texas," I tell her.

Amber gives me a look.

"What?" I say.

"I know where New Mexico is," she says, all huffy.

Mama waves her hand at us to stop. "I have just been invited to be the director of this new Montessori school. It's a great salary, and a wonderful opportunity for us to make a change."

"What about Kendell?" I ask

"Kendell?" Mama replies.

"Yes, Kendell, what about him, we can't leave him behind," I say trying hard to keep calm. "He's locked up in Dallas."

"Kendell left *us* behind long ago. And, as I said, this is an opportunity for us to move on." She looks at both of us for a reaction, but we are blank. "I understand this is not easy to take," she says, reaching for Amber's hand. "I know you like Happy Times, but you will like this school, too." Amber says nothing. "And it's not like we can't drive up to Dallas and visit Kendell."

Then Mama reaches for my hand but I move it away.

"I also like *my* school, and I like *my* life. No way you gonna take me outta here," I say, although deep inside I don't care about school, I don't care about moving, I only care about leaving my brother here on his own.

Mama takes a deep breath. "I understand, Leroy, I understand you have your life and you have Sharon but . . . "

Funny how little Mama knows about me. I wasn't even thinking about Sharon.

Mama continues, "This is our chance to experience something new. I've been reading about Taos and, well, even though it's a small town, it's a very important place for artists, perfect for you, Leroy. There are a lot of galleries and art classes and . . . "

"Taos?" says Amber, "That's a funny name. I like it, Taos. Taos. Taos. You say it, Leroy."

"Taos. Isn't that, like, in the middle of nowhere?" I ask.

"No it's in the middle of everything, close to Santa Fe, close to Albuquerque, close to . . . "

Taos, New Mexico. What the hell am I gonna do there? It's probably a super-white, boring town populated by senior citizens. Most likely they don't even have a mall where people like me go *cruising*. Yeah, there's probably no cruising in Taos. And I need that. That's all I got. That's the one thing that helps me survive. I'm like a vampire, but instead of living off of other people's blood, I survive by kissing guys I know I will never see again.

"And is it pretty?" Amber asks. But Mama doesn't say a word. She looks at me, waiting for my opinion, or trying to think of what else to add.

"And when is this gonna happen?" I ask.

"I want us to finish the school year, I think that's best. We'll go in the summer," she says and starts eating her food.

"So, in two months? You wanna move in two months?"

Mama nods with a crooked smile. She says nothing else.

So, this is it. We are leaving Dallas. We are moving to Taos and that's the end of it. The end of me.

amber

Well, we're moving. I'm excited! New home, new school, new friends, new everything. New, new, new, I can almost smell it. I'm sad because I like my friends, and my school, and my neighbors, and oh, my room, we just painted it! But, oh well.

Leroy, he is really mad. I can tell. You look at him in the eyes and you know he's boiling inside. He's not like Kendell. Kendell would have yelled and broken a couple of plates and glasses. Kendell would have said the F-word like, a ton of times. Leroy is different; you know he's angry because he stays quiet, drawing and drawing and drawing in his sketchbook. That's what he did after dinner. We cleaned the table and then he went to his room. Drawing and drawing and drawing.

He wouldn't even watch a movie with us, even though that is what we do on Fridays. We eat

Chinese take-out and watch a movie, the three of us. Unless he's out with his friends or Sharon.

I like Sharon, she's cool. She does my hair when she comes over. She doesn't have a little sister like me, and, well, what else is she going to do while Leroy pretty much ignores her? I don't understand how she doesn't see it. Or Mama. I don't understand how neither of them see that Leroy is gay. Only Kendell and I know about Leroy.

We gotta keep it a secret. That's what Kendell told me. I heard them talking one day. Kendell was telling him to be careful, that if Mama found out he was gay she would kill him. Leroy left and went to the mall with his friends, so I went to Kendell's room and asked him why he said that. I asked him if Leroy was gay.

I could see he was worried about telling me, but I said, "Believe it or not I can understand many things." He laughed at me first, but I guess when he saw how serious I was, he decided to explain.

"Come here, Amba girl," he said. Only my

family gets to call me that because I like it when people say my whole name, AMBER. Anyway, he sat me on his lap. "Leroy *is* gay, but you know Mama, she wouldn't like it. So we gotta keep it a secret, okay?"

"Promise," I said.

"Also, Leroy can't know about this, don't you tell him that you know."

"Why?"

"Because it would embarrass him or make him angry, I don't know, I just know he wouldn't like it. He'll tell you when he's ready."

"But there's nothing wrong with being gay; that's what Miss Robins tells us at school."

"I know, but . . . you just keep it a secret, okay? Do it for me."

"Yeah, yeah, I already promised." Kendell put me down, and I was heading out of his room, but I turned and asked, "What about Sharon?"

"What about her?"

"Does she know that Leroy is gay?"

"No, she doesn't. And we gotta keep it a secret from her, too."

"Oh, so it is all fake?"

"What is all fake?"

"Well, them, being sweethearts."

"I guess, but don't you open your mouth about it. I'm serious, Amber, if you say anything I will kick your ass."

I think that's the last time Kendell and I talked before he was taken away. I miss him sometimes.

* * *

Kendell was nice to us—me and Leroy. He's just not nice AT ALL with Mama. They used to fight all the time. I think they fight because they're so alike. I'm serious—Kendell is just as stubborn and grumpy as Mama. They like things done their way. Leroy and I are more alike, we are just quiet, sweet, funny creatures, or so I think. You yell at us, and we are crying for days. Okay, maybe not for days, but kinda. Maybe Leroy was supposed to be a girl, just like me, maybe that's why he's gay.

Anyway, what he told me was no surprise. Leroy is really handsome. And all gay men are really handsome, and they dress so nice. All my girlfriends at school say so. That gay men dress even better than women. My friends also say that both my brothers are handsome, but that Leroy is way handsomer. They've seen him when we have weekend activities at Happy Times and Mama brings him to help.

"Oh, Amber, that brother of yours. . . " they say.

"I have two brothers, you know," I remind them.

"Well, yes, but only one of them is mmhhhh!"

I always ask them who they're talking about, but I already know they mean Leroy. Kendell is good-looking, but you can see in his face that he's a lot of trouble. He is very nice with me, both of them are actually, but Kendell ain't nice with anyone else. Leroy, he is sweet with Mama, with Sharon, even with my friends and our neighbors. Leroy is a sweet pea. Are sweet peas gay?

I also hear our neighbors, the girls in apartment thirty-one, talking about Leroy in the laundry room. I even hear them saying "hi" and "hey" to him; he only smiles, like he's ashamed or something. And this, of course, makes the girls want him more. If only they knew what I know, that Leroy is gay.

But nobody knows he is gay because Leroy is, how do they say it on TV? Oh, yes, he is *in the closet.*

My brother, the chicken. I call him that in my mind, because he is afraid of everyone finding out about him. Poor Leroy! I sorta get it though. Mama is a real witch with them two—by the way, *witch* is my code for the B-word, which I'm not allowed to say or even think. Seriously, Mama is mean, and meaner with both of them. Like she doesn't love 'em.

One time, after hearing her arguing with my brothers, months and months before Kendell was taken away, I asked her, "Mama, why are you like that with Leroy and Ken?"

"Like what?"

"Mean. Why are you mean with them?"

"Am I? What about you? Am I mean with you, too?"

"No, just with them. Very mean, like the way you say your mama was with you."

"Oh, baby, it's not that I'm mean with them. When you are a mama yourself you will understand it."

"But I wanna understand it now."

"Amba girl, how can I explain this?"

"Just do, Mama. Just do."

"Well, you need to be different with men, because men are different. Men don't understand like women do. Women, we gotta watch our backs because men are a mess. Men. . . "

What Mama doesn't understand is that my brothers are not men. They are just boys. That day I told her exactly that. "They're not men, Mama, they just boys. And that ain't the same thing."

She looked at me, she gave me the same look

she gives my brothers when they don't do things the way she likes. The same look she gives to the principal of our school, Mrs. White, when she does something Mama doesn't like.

"You wouldn't understand," Mama said, "You're too young."

I wanted to say, "I ain't too young," but Mama would have said, "You are too." And then I would have said, "Well, they are too." But I didn't. With Mama you never win a fight, so there's no point. She is hardheaded, only she doesn't know it. Kendell is too, that is why he gets in so much trouble all the time.

Leroy and me, we are soft-hearted. Maybe that is why we are such chickens. Okay, no, I am not a chicken. Leroy is, but it's Mama's fault. She just won't talk to him. I think that's why Ken kept stealing things from people and getting into trouble. Miss Robins, my teacher, says that many of the things we do, we do them just for attention. Miss Robins is so smart.

Miss Robins doesn't get along with Mama all that much. Miss Robins is a lesbian and EVERYBODY knows it. But the reason Mama and Miss Robins don't get along is not only because Miss Robins is a lesbian, but because Mama is too much of a feminist, a man-heater almost. At least that is what I heard Miss Robins say today. I had forgotten about it; I wonder what she meant by "man-heater."

For some reason I knew better than to go and ask Mama if she believed she was too much of a feminist. So I go to Leroy's room and ask him.

"Hey, what's a feminist?"

Leroy is busy drawing. "What you say, Amba girl?" he asks me.

"A feminist, what's a feminist?" Leroy looks at me for like a second and then he goes back to his drawing. I know he's thinking what to tell me because he keeps scratching his forehead.

"Because I overheard Miss Robins saying to

Mr. Anderson that Mama was too much of a feminist," I say.

"Too much of a what?" Leroy asks me, pushing his drawing away.

"Too much of a feminist, almost a man-heater," I say.

He starts laughing and laughing and laughing. He tells me between laughs, "A man-*hater*, not a man-heater, Amber. That's probably what your teacher meant."

"Ohhh," I say, "But what does all that mean then?"

Leroy gets up and moves to Kendell's bed. "It seems like your Miss Robins and Mr. Anderson don't like Mama all that much, and they believe that Mama is . . . Mama is . . . too radical," Leroy says.

"Radical? What's that mean?" Leroy pulls closer to him and says,

"It means that Mama sometimes exaggerates. She is a little too mean when it comes to what she believes about men, so much that people, like your teacher, believe she hates men."

"Ohhhh, and that is why she is such a witch with you and Kendell."

"Amber, what did you say?"

"Witch, I said witch, and not the B-word. I never say the B-word."

"Well, don't say that word, either Amber. Mama hears you say it and she will spank your butt from here to Montana," Leroy says. "Now, go watch TV or do something, I'm busy."

Leroy goes back to his desk, but before I leave I tell him, "I love Mama, I love, love, love Mama. But I think she is sometimes unfair with people. I think it's unfair that she's mean to Miss Robins just because Miss Robins is gay. Do you know what gay is?"

Leroy ignores my question. He goes back to his drawing, and says, "Hey, do me a favor and close the door when you leave."

I'm disappointed. I guess I kinda wanted Leroy

to tell me something about being gay. Anything. I wanted him to share as much as he did with Kendell when he was here. But that ain't gonna happen because I am too young. I hate that everyone always tells me that. I can't wait to be a teenager so people start treating me like a grown-up and not like a little girl. In a few years I will be a teenager, maybe by then Kendell will be out, Leroy will stop hiding he's gay, and Mama—well, Mama will probably still be the same.

CHAPTER THREE
leroy

I'M SO MAD, AND WHEN I'M MAD THE ONLY THING that helps me is drawing. I'm mad at Mama because she wants us to move, because she wants to leave Kendell behind. Because she wants us to change our lives.

When I get mad at Mama I try to remind myself what she's gone through, and my anger calms a bit. Mama has done and learned everything the hard way, really.

Mama had to leave her parents' home when she got pregnant with Kendell at age sixteen. She worked her ass off for four years, and then she got herself through college to be an elementary school teacher.

In between classes and part-time jobs she found a boyfriend, and soon enough she was pregnant again, but that didn't stop her.

Not once did she stop working her ass off to give us as much as she could. Not even when she got pregnant for a third time. I think doing everything the hard way is why Mama tries to teach us everything the hard way, too. Except when it comes to Amber, she has a soft spot for her. And yeah, Amber does that to you, she is a sweetie, but just like Kendell, she doesn't bite her tongue when she has an opinion.

A couple of weeks ago, the three of us were watching a stupid romantic comedy. When it was over, Amber asked Mama how come she was still single. Mama only shrugged, but then Amber asked her, "And how come your boyfriends don't last?"

"Because they weren't good enough for me," Mama said, kinda as a joke, but kinda serious, too.

"Well, maybe the problem is that you don't know how to choose them," Amber barked.

Amber is right. Mama doesn't know how to choose men. Seriously, you can fill up a room with handsome, well-mannered, honest men, and Mama will go under the tables until she finds the one that ain't nothing like that. She has had a handful of boyfriends that together aren't worth a dime.

I don't know why she does that to herself. This is her pattern: she meets a guy, she starts dating the guy, then she brings the guy home for us to meet, and when we start liking him, she makes him disappear and starts talking shit about him.

Mama never talks shit about our fathers. We actually don't know much about them. This is what we do know: Kendell's father was eighteen when he and Mama started dating. He was nineteen when she got pregnant. He was twenty-one when he left.

My father and Mama met in college. They dated for a few months. Mama got pregnant. He moved in. They were together for almost three years. Kendell tells us he was actually nice, and that he loved Mama. Then one day he was gone.

Amber's father. The man we've never seen. Only thing we know about Amber's father is that he was probably white, because Amber is the color of honey.

Honey. That is actually the best word to describe Amber. My sister is like sweet, sweet honey. For now, at least. We'll see what happens as she gets older. Hopefully she won't turn as grumpy as Mama.

When Kendell was taken away, Mama and I felt a mix of anger, sadness, and bitterness. Amber was crying a lot. She gave him a hug and promised him that she would take care of us, she would take care of our secrets and everything else.

Amber is like a wise old woman disguised in the body of a girl. When she was six or seven she had a play date at home with one of her friends.

"Hey Amber, where's your dada, how come you don't have one?" the girl asked her.

"Not all dadas live with their kids."

"Yeah, but that's called divorce," her friend said. "But you still have a dada, even though he lives somewhere else. Tell me about yours."

"Well, I'll tell you one thing, we didn't divorce my dad. We decided I didn't need him or his last name."

"We?"

"Yeah, Mama and I. That's why I'm Amber Davis."

"All mamas need dadas."

"Hey, did you come to play, or did you come to talk about the dada I don't have?"

I think the reason why Amber's so smart is because Mama was older when she had her, she wasn't a teenager with a baby in her arms. She was already working as a teacher's assistant, she had gone to college, and had figured out that nothing bad happens to a kid who eats mud cakes, and that it's even healthier if they do, it's healthier if they are allowed to be curious, if they are raised not to be afraid.

Amber also got it easier because by the time she

was in kindergarten, Mama was already a certified Montessori instructor. Our sister goes to the school where Mama works. This school operates under the philosophy that every child is a natural learner, and that it's very important to let them ask, explore, and learn at their own rhythm. Amber is creative, obedient, smart, and curious. She questions everything, which can be good and bad, of course.

If I had gone to a Montessori school, just like Amber does, I am sure I would have had no problem admitting I was gay and being accepted as such. Maybe if Mama had gone to a Montessori school, or if she had been an instructor before we were born, our lives would have been very different, or at least, she would be able to accept the fact that she has one gay son.

mama

Taos will suit us; I just hope *we* suit Taos. I know this will be a huge change for all of us as a family, but change is good. "If you don't like something, change it." That's what Maya Angelou said at that conference I attended a few years ago, and Maya Angelou is always right. I remember hearing her and thinking, "She is talking to me, she is telling me to change, she's telling me that if I can't change something, I am the one who needs to change." But I didn't do shit, and I guess now I'm paying the price for that.

I'm not worried about Amber, God bless her, that girl and her resilience. It's just fascinating to see her react to whatever God places in front of her. I like seeing her in the schoolyard. While the rest of her classmates wait in line to have a turn on the slide or on the swings Amber stays behind. She avoids the line and simply sits on a bench entertaining herself with a book or watching an insect. It's like she knows that the slide or the swings will always be there, waiting for her turn to use them.

But Leroy, he does worry me. I knew he wasn't gonna like the idea of moving. I knew he was going to get mad quietly, as he always does. I know he won't fight my decision; still, he will carry the burden of the change by himself. Like he always does. I don't understand him sometimes. I wish he had gotten involved in sports as much as Kendell did when he was younger. That would have helped him develop his social skills. It's just that he is so, so quiet. You never know what he's thinking.

I have tried to understand him through his drawings and paintings, I have tried to read his mind through the lines, figures and colors he uses, but he remains a mystery. Of course, I'm proud of what he does. I love the idea of him becoming a successful artist, and not because he knows how to hold a ball, a microphone, or a gun. I just wish, I just wish I knew what goes on in that head of his.

* * *

Change, that's what my Leroy needs. Change. A new start. A new place.

I blame it on the city. This city has brought so much trouble to our family. Yes, I blame the city for the way Kendell has turned out, the city and its *unjust* justice system. If the city hadn't decided to punish Kendell with juvenile detention because he bought a stolen bike—without knowing it was stolen—his life would have turned out so different. Those months in Juvenile changed him forever.

I am not stupid. I understand that he is his own victimizer. It's like the city did part of the job and he has unceasingly done the rest to ruin his future. He became such a troublemaker after Juvenile, and there was so little I could do about it. I am not like those mothers who blame themselves for whatever their children do, or perhaps I am, but I don't do it all the time. I know better than that. Anyway, I have done nothing but my best to give a good life to all of my kids, even though I had no one to teach me how to be a mother. Oh, but no matter how much you try, kids always find a way to mess it all up. That's what Kendell did and I don't want Leroy or Amber to follow in his footsteps.

With Kendell I've had it.

I wonder what Leroy actually thinks of his brother. I wonder if he feels the need to be a bad boy also. I mean, teenagers and trouble come together after all. I am sure Leroy has done things behind my back, things with his so-called "friends." Maybe they have convinced him to drink, or even worse, to smoke pot. He spends too much time out at the mall or at the park, and what else do teenagers do at the mall or at the park in this city? Truth is that if he's doing any of these things, he's being real careful because not once has he ever come home late, or drunk, or smelling like weed.

"I'm with my friends, Mama," he says. Friends my ass. Those kids, whoever they are, are probably no good for Leroy. Friends call, friends get involved in your life, friends are there when you need them the most. And these kids? Well, hear me out, these kids have never called him to see how he is or anything like that. And I know Leroy is having a hard time with Kendell and everything. So where are they now that Leroy needs them? Imaginary friends, that's what they seem to be.

That's not my case. I may not have all that many friends, but the ones I have are caring, supportive, understanding. Take Liz, for example. She's the one who told me about this position in Taos; she's the one who convinced me to apply. "Restart your life, get out of Dallas, move to Taos. Give yourself and your kids a chance to experience something new."

Liz's words tempted me. I read all about Taos and she's right; I can restart our lives in this place. Taos is what we need as a family. I mean, Amber's resilience is amazing and I am certain that she will adapt easily. Leroy is not as easy when it comes to adapting, but I think he has the most to gain from life in Taos. Taos is filled with artists, galleries, studios; it will simply be perfect for a young artist like him.

I don't know where he got it from, his drawing and paintings are simply beautiful. It doesn't matter if he does something as abstract as he did in that acrylic painting about the Dallas World Aquarium, or something as simple as the charcoal-sketched hands he did using Amber as a model. Leroy is an artist. I believe in him, and there's nothing I want more than for him to pursue his dreams. He's going to be big, I know it, I just know it.

Who knows, maybe one of those artists who live in Taos may even "adopt" him and mentor him.

Leroy is pure sense and sensitivity. Sometimes more sensitivity than sense, I must say. When he was a child he would cry about every little thing; he would erupt in these gigantic tantrums. Now that he's older, the tantrums are gone, but not the sensitivity. I understand why that girl Sharon fought so hard to get his attention, and Leroy doesn't seem to care. Sometimes I think he is from another planet. He's different from any of the kids his age.

Sharon is such a nice girl, she might be Leroy's only true friend. She calls him all the time, stops by, convinces him to go out. Poor Leroy, I know he still is broken-hearted about his brother, even though he doesn't say it. Like I said, he keeps everything to himself, the good and the bad.

I'm all broken up too, but I am tired of cleaning up Kendell's messes. The way I see it, I got one job as a mom, get my kids ready for the world. And if I could not do that for Kendell, I still have Leroy and Amber to look after. Liz is right, Dallas has become a difficult place to live, and Taos will give us a chance to re-group. Who knows? Maybe Leroy will end up liking the place, and find whatever it is he's looking for.

I just wanna build a different life for him, different from the one Kendell chose, different from the rest of the kids around us. If only this would help him to open up with me, to communicate with me, to share with me everything in his life, like what he does when he goes to the mall for hours. Oh, Leroy.

CHAPTER FOUR
leroy

I'M GETTING READY FOR BED WHEN SHARON TEXTS ME and says: How was the family meeting, baby?

Heavy

Tell me bout it

Not now. I'm tired. I'm going to bed now.

You should come to MY bed

There's no way to deal with Sharon's . . . Sharon's harassment, yes, that's what it is, harassment. She's worse than a dog in heat, seriously. I have no clue how I'm gonna deal with her tomorrow. I can't keep playing "good boy" with her. She wants sex and if I don't do anything about it, who knows what she'll do. Things are okay the way they are.

Well, no, they really aren't. Who am I trying to fool? Things with Sharon are not okay. Our whole relationship is a lie. The only way things could work between us would be if Sharon had a chest instead of boobs. A dick instead of, ugh. Can't even think of Sharon's *down there* without feeling sick.

Oh, Sharon, what am I going to do? You are great, yes, you are. I don't want to lose you; you bring so much sense to my life. I'm serious, I may not be in love with her, but I love her, and she's like the closest friend I've ever had. She's smart, at least she is when sex isn't taking over everything in her mind.

This is all Nona and Jill's fault. Ever since they had sex with their boyfriends, they've been bullying her to do the same. Virgin Sharon they call her, or so Sharon says. I tell her to ignore them. They aren't her friends if they're like that. But Sharon ignores me. She wants to fit in, that's all. And who am I to blame her? I'm doing the same thing, trying to fit in.

I hate how we are both craving approval. In a way, we are perfect for each other. She's the brains and I'm the emotions in this relationship. When I cry over a movie or a book, she says nothing. She stands there, holding my hand or rubbing my shoulder. Only when she sees that I feel better does she joke and says things like, "Who's the girlfriend here?" She wipes my tears and kisses me softly.

Sharon is gonna go crazy when I tell her about Taos. Hell, *I* am going crazy just thinking about it. It's already too hard to have this sorta double life I have here in Dallas, imagine how it would be in a town with like twenty-five inhabitants.

Double life. I am making it sound as if I really have a life in which I am openly gay. Not even close. I am just one of those guys hiding here and there, waiting for another closeted, horny gay guy willing to get some action in a public restroom. I am so pathetic.

* * *

Sharon texts me again:

Hello? You still there, my baby, are you sleeping already?

Nah, I can't. There's so much on my mind

You know you can talk to me, right? Is this about Kendell?

No, for the first time it's not about Kendell. It's my fucking mom

Whoa, what's wrong, babe? You never call her that. U sure u are OK?

It's nothing. It's everything. I just can't explain.

Come to my place, we can talk about it

Are you serious? It's kinda late

I am here for you, talk to me. Just come and we will sit down and talk about whatever it is

I don't know...

Come. If you don't wanna talk about it that's fine, we'll just watch a stupid movie and eat ice cream. If that doesn't make you feel better, there's always making out

Ha ha

I'm not taking no for an answer. Ask your mom or sneak out, I don't care, but I wanna see you at my place in 30 minutes. OK?

OK

Oh, Sharon. She's so great to me. I wish I could love her the same way she loves me. I wish I could give her more. Sometimes I think I'd be lost without her. She's the only one who understands me and everything in my family. She's the only one who helps me; she keeps me *straight*.

sharon

I wonder what's wrong with Leroy. I mean, he's always been a bit weird, but well, lately he's been . . . I don't know. His mother is a piece of work, seriously. Sometimes she treats him as if he were the worst of the worst. Same with Kendell, but well, Kendell can be a little too much, I'll give her that. But not Leroy, he's a great student, and he's talented. He's a good boy. Even with me, he wouldn't touch me.

I honestly don't understand him sometimes. Like today, when I told him my parents were away and invited him to spend the night. Who wouldn't take the chance of sleeping over at his girlfriend's place without ANY interruption? I know this proves he loves me and respects me. If he didn't, he would have already had sex with me just to tell everyone at school about it. That's how boys are. Not Leroy though. He's different, and that's what I love, love,

LOVE about him. But that's also what I hate, hate, HATE about him.

Yeah, Leroy is too much of a good boy.

Listen to me, complaining that my boyfriend is a good boy when at school all everyone is talking about is that stupid Tina Jones, who has been sleeping with Danny Freeman, and was recorded on his phone, blowing him. Can you believe that? If I were Tina I would kill Danny with my bare hands.

Once I offered Leroy a blowjob. Not that I'm an expert, but I mean how hard can it be? It's just that I was under the impression that all guys like blowjobs, and a blowjob is not real sex, right? Anyway, Leroy almost choked. "Would you let me blow you?" I said, all well-mannered and shit with my wording. Leroy looked at me as if I had invited him to rob a bank—no, worse—he looked at me as if I had just opened his fly in public. "What did you just say?" he asked, his face all tomato-red.

We were at home. My parents were out. We

were watching a movie and making out. Okay, maybe we were just sorta making out, because even though Leroy is the kind of guy who caresses you, holds your hand and tells you sweet words, he isn't all that much into touchy-touchy. He rejected me, of course, moved my hand from his lap and then he told me what he always says, "I'm with you because you are special, and because you are special I respect you." My first reaction was to look at him, put his hand between my legs and say, "Come on, let's have some fun."

Leroy stood up, took his things and left. I swear, sometimes I think he is the girlfriend. This probably makes me the boyfriend, a very horny boyfriend, of course. But now he's coming over. I know, I know, he's coming to talk, but who knows? Maybe I'll get lucky. I wonder what his mother did this time. I swear it, that woman doesn't value Leroy.

He is just perfect, the perfect student, the perfect boy, the perfect boyfriend.

Maybe too perfect. And that's why we haven't done it.

I hate being the only virgin left. All of my friends have had sex. Take Nona and Jill, for example. Nona did it with her ex-boyfriend a few weeks ago, and she doesn't talk about anything else—she also doesn't do anything else but get laid every time she can. Jill has been doing it with this kid from the community college she met online. I know I'm making them sound like *hoes*, but they aren't. A girl who has casual sex is not a *ho*, she's just a girl willing to explore life.

That's what I want to do with Leroy, explore life. He'd be awesome.

This is how I picture it: he will kiss me softly, he will caress me. He will take care of me. He's gonna be sweet and tender. He would not hurt me, Leroy would never hurt me. And then, then we will be closer than ever. We will be the perfect couple.

I know he wouldn't tell everybody about it, like other guys do. One: because he isn't like that; and two: because, let's be honest, Leroy doesn't have all that many friends. He's a weirdo, my boyfriend. But he's *my* weirdo. And weirdo or not, he is far better than any of my friends' boyfriends or crushes.

Maybe I'm the one who's a weirdo; no, no, maybe I'm a ho-weirdo! Ha ha! Oh well, I don't feel ashamed about asking my boyfriend to have sex. But I'm a bit ashamed that he keeps saying no. Wait, no, he hasn't said no, but he hasn't said yes, either. It's like he has me in this limbo, a sexless limbo.

I have tried pretty much everything to seduce him. Nothing seems to work. Last weekend, when we went to the movies, I went bra-less and wore a cute Banana Republic t-shirt, that kind with spandex. My perkiness was out in the open. What did Leroy do? Nothing. The guy who gave us the popcorn stared at my happy nipples and undressed me with his eyes. Not Leroy.

What's worse is that the more difficult things are with him, the more I want to get laid. I'm sure that if I was his brother's girlfriend, I would not have these issues. Kendell is more . . . normal. I've only seen him a couple of times, but that was enough to realize that he is the thug that all girls want. Seriously!

I love Leroy, don't get me wrong, but Kendell seems, I dunno, dangerous. Once I had a dream, this ultra-super-wet-dream in which Kendell and I were making out in my room. I have had fantasies with Leroy, but not dreams.

My only dream is to marry him. Imagine me marrying my high school sweetheart? I know that seems silly, I should want a college degree. But I could get the two, the degree and the husband.

The perfect life. That's what I want.

Anyway, if there's someone to "blame" for Leroy's asexual behavior it's his mom. She got pregnant when she was like sixteen, and look at her now, three kids later and still a single mom. I bet she brainwashed him about the dangers of pleasure. Just because she fucked up and didn't know about the existence of birth control doesn't mean that we will end up doing the same. Anyway, even if we *did* fuck up, it would be OUR problem, not hers. Plus, Leroy would never bail out on me, like some guys do. No, he wouldn't.

Leroy, he's different.

I wonder what I have to do to get in his pants. Maybe I need to get him drunk, like Danny did with Tina, only I wouldn't film him, at least not without his permission, ha ha.

Geez, I'm such a ho.

Uh, it's late. He'll be here any minute now. I have to change, I should put on my PJs, and pretend I am just in my comfy mode. Comfy-sexy mode, of course. Ah, Sharon, you are so, so, selfish, what if he's really feeling like shit and I'm here only thinking about sex? I swear I'm a big ho.

sharon and leroy

"Hey Babe! So, what happened?"

"What can I say? My mother. Again." Leroy plopped down on the couch.

"Oh, sweetie. Here, let me give you a hug."

"Sharon, I hate her, I just hate her."

"Don't say that. Wait, no, do it, do say that, get it out of your system, come on, let's go to the kitchen. Let's get you something."

"Sure. So, what were you doing?"

"Before I started molestexting you, you mean? Nothing really, I was bored to death. Hey, why don't we switch that ice cream for something more . . . ?"

"Something more what?"

"Something more *amusing.*"

"What do you mean?"

"Wait, just a second, let me look for it. My

mother keeps hiding this from me. But she can't fool me."

"Hiding what, Sharon?"

"This! Look at it, a beautiful bottle of vodka. We only have to mix it with ice and cranberry juice, or do you like apple juice?"

"Vodka? Are you serious?"

"Why not?"

"Wait, but why did your mother hide the vodka from you, oh, wait, is this because of that night with Nona and Jill?"

"Yup. No matter how many times I've apologized, she says I can't be trusted."

"Well, she has a point."

"Shut up. So, are you in or out?"

"I dunno, Sharon."

"Come on, Leroy, don't be a party pooper. Besides, it will help you relax."

"Fine, but just one drink."

"Cool. Pass those glasses? Now tell me, what

happened with your mother, you wanna talk about it or . . . "

"Not really. Not now."

"Got it."

"Hey, I think that's way more vodka than it's supposed to be."

"Says who? Hey, you want me to tell you the latest news about Jill and her college boy?"

"That still going on?"

"Well, kinda, you won't believe this. College boy asked Jill if she be willing to be in a threesome."

"Wait, what?"

"Yup."

"She said no, right?"

"That's where you are wrong, honey, she said yes. And get this, the threesome involved this other guy."

"Holy shit, what did she do? She said yes?"

"Of course not. I mean, at first she did, she is such a ho, but Nona advised her otherwise."

"Wow, Nona giving wise advice? That's new."

"Here's your drink. Cheers. Gimme a kiss . . . You like it? Is it too strong?"

"A little, I'll just put in some more juice. Okay, keep going with the story."

"Oh, yeah, well, now Jill is broken-hearted because according to Nona, if a man wants a threesome with two girls, that means he's just fun-kinky. But if a man wants a threesome with a girl and a boy, then, that means something else."

"It does?"

"Yup. It means the guy is more into guys than girls."

Leroy coughs.

"Leroy, you okay?"

"Yeah . . . it's just, this thing is still too strong. So y'all think he's gay?"

"Of course, he's gay, why would he wanna be in bed with another man if he wasn't?"

"Maybe he's bisexual."

"Oh, come on, bisexuals are a joke. He's a fag, a fag who is afraid of being a fag and that's why he bangs a younger girl and tries to convince her into a threesome. He's just a fag who pretends he isn't . . . Leroy, you sure you are okay?"

"Yeah, it's just this thing."

"Here, let me pour some more juice and ice. Anyway, now Jill is on the verge of suicide, poor thing. I tell you Leroy, she can be so stupid. I mean how could she not see it? No wonder this guy didn't wanna hang out with us, he didn't wanna meet any of Jill's friends."

"Why?"

"Because we would find out, one way or another, duh! Hey, let's go to the living room, wanna watch some TV?"

"Sure."

"That guy is an asshole. I mean, Jill was all crazy about him, she talked about him all the time."

"What if, what if he really cared about her, what if he really likes her?"

"Oh, come on, you don't think that, do you? If

a guy asks a girl to go to bed with someone else, woman or man, that means he's not that into you."

"But that doesn't necessarily mean he's gay, maybe he's just, I don't know, exploring."

"Come on, would you ask *me* to do something like that? Well, first we would have to be sexually active, which we aren't."

"Sharon."

"I'm kidding, I'm just kidding. But seriously, let's say we were already having sex like *everybody else in school*. Would you ask me to have sex with you and someone else?"

"No, of course not."

"You see?"

"But maybe . . . "

"Okay, okay, maybe he's not gay, or not *that* gay. But there's something fishy about him."

"I guess."

"If I were Jill, I would kill him with my bare hands. No, better, I would tell EVERYONE about him, that'd teach him not to mess with me. Hey, did you already finish your drink?"

"Yeah, well, it was . . . I was thirsty I guess."

"Do you want another one?"

"No."

"Oh come on, you know you want it, and I promise I'm talking about the drink."

* * *

"Here. Cheers. Mmhh, you smell good. I wanna bite you."

"Sharon, come on."

"What? What's wrong with me wanting to be close to you, Leroy? You're here, and you and I know *why* you're here."

"Baby, no, we've talked about this."

"I know. I know, but I have to be honest, Leroy. I want you. I want you so bad. And I know you want me too. That's why you keep running away from me."

"Running away from you? When?"

"All the time. You and your PDA thing."

"PDA?"

"Yes, public display of affection, oh my god, sometimes you are so slow. Come get close to me."

leroy

Sharon and I were talking in the kitchen, then we went to the living room. First we were sitting on the sofa, and then after she got me the second or third drink she sat on my lap and started playing with my hair. I felt uncomfortable, but at the same time I liked it. I felt loved. I closed my eyes and let her fingers caress my hair, my face, my ears, my neck.

Then she started kissing me. My eyes closed. Her tongue found her way inside my mouth. First softly, then not so much. I dropped my glass and a thin trickle of vodka and juice began to spill on the carpet. "Forget about it," she said and kept kissing me.

By then she was all on me. Her legs each on one side. She was mounting me. Sharon was kissing me so hard that I felt a tingling in my spine. Then, all of a sudden I was hard, really hard. Was it Sharon or the alcohol? *I should stop*, I told myself, but didn't. I pulled my fingers through her hair, caressed her back. My hands on her round, perfect ass. It was the ass of a girl, yes, but I still wanted it. I wanted her. I knew I was making a mistake, but I didn't have the energy to stop it. I went along with it.

Sharon reached for my waistband and drew me into her body.

Between kisses I tried to stop her and said, "Hey, Sharon, we shouldn't be doing this, not now." But she wouldn't listen. "It's okay, I want it just as bad as you do." Everything was fuzzy. I was inside her. I was inside a woman and it felt weird. I closed my eyes and pictured myself in a different position and with a different person. I picture myself with a guy.

I was careful not to come inside her. I stayed by her side. I cuddled her. I caressed her hair. "Leroy, I love you," she said. All I could do was kiss her forehead and keep her in my arms.

It was a mistake. It was all a mistake. I am such an asshole. I feel so dirty.

sharon

I can't believe we did it. We actually did it. At first I felt like a guy, you know, a guy pushing his girlfriend to get laid with him. But I know that if I hadn't gotten him drunk, he wouldn't have dared have sex with me.

I was a little worried, I mean, we had no condoms, but he took care of that. It was kinda disgusting if you ask me. And messy.

I can't lie, it hurt. It hurt a lot. But after a while, the pain was gone and I enjoyed it as he moved inside me, he was breathing on my face, he was sweating, his eyes closed as if he was embarrassed to see me or be seen by me.

When it was over, he was so sweet and wonderful. He cuddled with me, caressed my hair and my face. He kissed me on the forehead and I felt complete.

I am so lucky.

CHAPTER FIVE
leroy

I DON'T CARE ABOUT OUR APARTMENT OR ABOUT MY school . . . hell, I don't care about anything. But I feel like shit for leaving Sharon now. It was hard to tell her we were moving.

I told her a few days after we had sex. She was mad at first. "Why didn't you tell me that the night you came over?" she said. I had no answer, but she had one for me. "That's why you did it with me? Because you knew you were leaving, because you knew that was our only chance, our last chance?" Then she kissed me. She cried and cried. I cried with her, but not for her.

I feel like I ended up acting like every other guy

in school. Man, she didn't deserve that, but I guess that was the one good thing about moving. I don't have to do it with her again. I don't know how I pulled that off. Sex was . . . arghh . . . I don't even wanna think about it.

I can't believe I had sex with a girl. I can't believe I had sex with Sharon. I can't believe I left Dallas and the last time I had sex it was with a girl, because who knows when I'm gonna get laid again? Taos means no cruising, Taos means lying even more. Taos means a life I don't want.

* * *

WHY DID WE HAVE TO MOVE?! I just don't get it. No matter how many times Mama explained her reasoning, no matter how artsy this place is and how I will be the main beneficiary of this change, blah, blah, blah . . . WHY DID WE HAVE TO MOVE? I will hate this tiny super-white-granola town, I know I will.

It's only been a week and I already know every-thing about it: (1) every other building has a story to tell about the past, (2) all its food is based on red chilies, green chilies, or both, (3) there are two heritages, the native American and the Spanish, (4) it is not a city, it is not a town, it's what they call a *pueblo*, which is basically Spanish for small-small-small town, (5) there are eight restaurants, one of them is a McDonald's and the other one is a New Mexican version of McDonald's and it's called Blake's, (6) there are two supermarkets and three pharmacies, (7) there are many art galleries, which are actually kinda cool, (8) and that's it.

I'm using this list to write a letter to Kendell, at least that will make him laugh. Kendell. Just thinking about his face when Mama told him we were moving makes me wanna cry. He didn't say anything, which is new because normally he would have exploded. He just simply nodded and asked me and Mama to write and call as much as we could. "Tell Amber to keep sending me those postcards she makes," he said. I'm sure he felt betrayed. I'm sure he feels we left him behind. As if he wasn't part of the family anymore.

I don't think we will ever finish unpacking. Let me rephrase that, *I* will never finish unpacking. I brought way more shit than Mama did. I should have listened to her and donated some of my stuff to Goodwill, and some to the trashcan.

Instead, I have to unpack clothes, books, shoes, old CDs, spelling-bee medals, clay figures, butterfly collection number one, and butterfly collection number two.

Everything I own is boxed and waiting for me to make a move. Just like my life. I try not to think about it, because it's embarrassing, but I am boxed. The real me is inside a box, a box that I decided to store away when I was a kid. My spirit is so well packed and deep in a closet that there will be a day when not even I will know how to find it. How to find myself.

I'll be lost.

I am lost.

Forget about cruising, forget about finally coming out, none of that is gonna happen, not in this town.

* * *

Mama comes in my room and says,

"Are you done?"

"Of course not," I reply. "There are too many things. So . . . what if I unpack just the basics and then put the rest of the boxes in the closet?" Mama looks at me, the way she does when someone says something absolutely stupid.

"Leroy Bartlett, do that and I will whup your ass, I promise. You will never see . . . "

" . . . the end of it, I know, I know, Mama. But look, most of this is for winter, we won't need it 'til who knows when?"

"Fine. Leave whatever you won't be using right now in the boxes. But put away all the rest, ALL

THE REST. And hurry up. In an hour you have that job interview I got you, remember?"

"Job interview?"

"Yes, Leroy, at that coffee shop. Don't pretend you don't remember."

"Mama, do I really need to get a job?"

"Hell, yes, this is the best way for you to get to know the town, meet people, and be independent."

"I don't need no job for that. I will make friends once classes starts."

"Oh, no. I know you and you will be locked up here for the rest of the summer, no way."

"What if that's what I want? I wanna focus on my painting and drawing."

"You'll still have time for that, it's not like you will be working all day every day."

"But . . . "

"But nothing. I set this all up for you. Now, please, finish and take a shower. You need to look nice and clean."

When Mama leaves, I turn around, a bunch of

boxes stare at me. Many of them have my name on them, but there are a few with Kendell's name written on them. That's what he is to us now, a name on a box. Three boxes in the middle of a room that say Kendell. Man, I miss him. At least back home we were able to see him a couple of times a month. Now, who knows when we'll be visiting him again?

I pick one of his boxes and open it. All of a sudden I hear Mama's voice behind me,

"Hey, I know this is hard. Believe me, it's hard for me, too. Moving, changing, starting all over, not easy, not easy at all. Don't think too much about it, though, honey," Mom says before adding, "But DO IT already."

"I will, I will, I will." I tell her.

* * *

Once, Kendell tried to convince me to come out to Mama. This was before he went to jail, of course.

"Dude, you gotta tell her!" he said.

I protested. "She will probably want to kill me!"

He looked me in the eyes. "Yeah, at first, but eventually she will understand, or sorta. And if she doesn't, you can always be a runaway," he replied.

I should have listened to him, I should have come out to her a long time ago, because now is really not the time at all for this. Mom already has enough on her plate, she doesn't need to put up with a gay son, no she doesn't.

I put away Kendell's boxes, the winter stuff, and pretty much everything else; I'm not in the mood for this. I move around the bed, the night table, to try to make my room look like an actual room. Once I'm done I focus on my desk.

I take out all my art materials: charcoal set, watercolor pencils, canvas, paper, brushes, palette, sponges, everything. I divide my desk in two and organize my painting accessories on one side and my drawing accessories on the other.

I have a print of my favorite Georgia O'Keeffe

painting; I put it on the wall right in front of my desk. It's an oil on canvas of a river.

* * *

Mama drives me to the coffee shop.

"Pay attention, cause you gonna walk home on your own," she says. "You need to learn your way around."

I listen to her and tell myself, "Oh yeah, because one could get lost in this shitty little town."

Mama turns right, left, and then she goes straight for like seven minutes. Old buildings, galleries, Mexican restaurants, convenience stores that seem to have been there since the civil war, more old houses, and then in the middle of a parking lot, surrounded by trees, I see it: The Spot Coffee Shop.

The building is like an old wooden cottage painted red and with a big green door. Outside, a woman with the reddest hair I've ever seen sits cross-legged on the porch, reading a newspaper. A huge yellow dog lays at her feet.

"That's the owner," Mama says. "Good luck!" she whispers as I climb out of the car.

As I get closer, the dog stands up, barks at me, and wags its tail. The red-headed woman smiles, stands up, and greets me. "You must be Leroy," she says. "I'm Samantha, but you can call me Sam." She invites me inside the coffee shop. She smells like cinnamon and vanilla. She turns to me and says, "Welcome to The Spot, let me show you around."

samantha

After the interview is over, I show the kid around. He seems to be a nice kid, just like his mother promised.

Out on the porch we have a few tables, but it's summer, so no one wants to be there during the day. Only me, I guess. This was an old house, so as you can see what used to be the living room and the dining room are now open spaces for our customers. Make sure all tables are clean all the time.

This small room was some sort of studio; I made it into our storage room. I'm a little bit OCD so everything here has a place and a tag. There's no way you'll get confused. My storage is like Taos, small and easy to understand.

Something *very* important is that the storage room must be closed at all times. Remind me to make you a key, okay? The thing is Clara is a big girl, but from time to time she gets crazy, she sneaks in and bites whatever she can reach. So, let's keep temptations out of her way. Clara is my dog. You saw her, isn't she a cutie? Clara, Clara? Oh, she must be in the freshest corner of the place resting, that's all she does these days. Clara, honey, you there? She's getting old, I think she's going deaf.

Anyway, for now I think you can help cleaning tables, taking orders, and little by little we will train you to do something else, how does that sound?

Now, follow me. This is the counter, obviously, on the right we keep sugar, milk, honey, and spoons. Make sure there's always fresh milk. We place the pastries in this cabinet here. The pastries come at seven forty-five a.m., so if you get a morning shift, make sure you are here before then. Linda, our pastry chef, doesn't like to wait. Once she got so mad that she didn't bring deliveries for almost a week, just because we made her wait ten minutes. Always offer her coffee, she'll say no, but she likes the attention. Place the pastries here, I'll show you later how we serve each one. I use chocolate or whipped cream for presentation. Lots of chocolate and lots of whipped cream, I don't know what it is with people in Taos, but everyone here has a sweet tooth.

Why? I don't know, maybe because of the weather. See, Taos is all about extremes. It is either too hot or too cold, so I guess people here need a treat to survive the weather.

This is our coffee station. It must be clean at all times. Martin will teach you how to use our espresso machine, a bit temperamental—our machine, not Martin. I'll introduce you to him when he comes back. He can tell you more about this whole place, he pretty much runs it for me. I have two other kids, Lynn and Mike. You'll meet them in a bit.

Your mother told me you are an artist. Oh, god, I made you blush. No, don't say you aren't one, if you draw or paint on a daily basis then you are one. So I would love you to help us out with these walls. I have some paintings and photographs in my office. Come on, I want you to take a look at them and help me decide what to hang on our walls. No, don't worry, I'm sure you'll do a wonderful job.

Here they are, they are framed and everything as you can see. Go ahead, look at them, take your time.

* * *

So, how do you like Taos so far?

Oh, boy, you really don't know how to lie, do you? Your lips say, 'Taos is okay,' but your eyes say, 'I hate it.' Ha ha. Oh, change that face. It's okay if you don't like it now. I mean, you are coming from an actual city, after all. But, listen to me, Taos is the kind of place that grows into you. I know, I know it's very small, and pretty much in the middle of nowhere, but there is such diversity in this town! It's a small community—no, it's more like a big family. But not like the dysfunctional kind in which there is a crazy member that makes life miserable for everybody. No, this is a family in which everybody is a little crazy, so no one has time to be miserable.

Everybody helps everybody. Everybody respects everybody. Everybo . . .

Yes, that woman in the picture is me. Can you believe how young and beautiful I was? Yes, that's Germany, have you been there? I lived there almost ten years with my husband, back when I wanted to believe that I liked men, which was a zillion years ago. What? No, no don't worry, I don't mind explaining, I'm too old to be shy about my life. You see, I got married when I was nineteen years old, and when you are nineteen years old you know nothing. How old are you? Seventeen? Oh well, you know less than nothing then, ha ha. I'm joking, kid.

No, really, don't look so embarrassed, I don't mind talking about me. I am my favorite topic. Anyway, it's quite simple actually. Listen:

I met my husband when I was in college and he was in grad school. He got a job in Germany, and the only way my parents would let me be with him in Germany was if we were married. So I got married; I was a bored and boring wife, but then I met this fabulous woman, and I completely fell for her. I left it all: Germany, husband, and pets, and came back to the U.S. to follow the person I believed was the love of my life. We lived all over the country. She was a painter and I was a waitress, and we lived off her grant money and our love. Until one day there were no more grants, or love. We had lived in Albuquerque for two years, the happiest years of our relationship, so when she left me, I decided to come back to New Mexico. By then my parents had died. In case you're wondering, no I did not kill them by becoming a lesbian. It was a topic we never discussed. They left me money, lots of it, and since I had almost a Ph.D. in waitressing, well, I decided it was time to be my own boss and I opened my place.

* * *

Leroy, kid, change that face, if I'm not embarrassed about telling my whole life to a total stranger, then you shouldn't be either. I have lived a full life, I love it all, the good, the bad, and the worst. It all made me who I am now, and I like who I am now. I believe that's one of the biggest issues people have, they don't like themselves, they don't accept themselves. How can you like life or how can you accept life if you don't start with your own?

Oh, look at me, I'm overwhelming you with my ideas. Now, tell me about you. I love knowing everything about my employees. Wait, no, no, let me learn about you on my own. Let's sit here. Do you want something to drink? Let me get you an iced tea. Today's flavor is Jamaica.

Here it is, I hope you like it. I don't have my tarot now, but maybe one of these days I can do a reading on you?

You are telling me no one has ever read you the tarot? Oh, you'll love it. I call it therapeutic readings. You see, it's not like I'll tell you the future, I will tell you about your past and present, so you can learn about yourself, and learn about the challenges you are facing and that you are unable to see.

Come on, don't be scared, I am no witch. We don't have to do the tarot now, just let me look at your hands. Let's figure out who Leroy is. Tell me when and where you were born. I am a master when it comes to astrology.

You are a Pisces! I love Pisces. They are so intuitive. It's funny how helpful they can be with big, complicated problems, their own or other people's; but when it comes to basic stuff, they just get lost. I bet it took you ages to learn how to tie your own shoes. Pisces have an 'old soul,' they look into the souls of people. They are a realm of tranquility, unlike Aries who are all about war. Your mother is Aries? Oh my god, how do you survive her? She is probably all about getting things done at once, and you, well, you take your time. Mmhmm, I see I've hit a nerve, ha ha.

What else? Well, Pisces have a hard time keeping

relationships. Pisces men tend to choose the wrong women. And well, Pisces gay men, those are worse because, not only do they choose women for partners, they. . . are you okay? Leroy?

Oh, my. You're gay, aren't you? Oh sweetie, I am so sorry, me and my big mouth, look, I made you uncomfortable, I didn't mean to, believe me. I never learn.

Please, don't go. Let's talk. Here, sit down. I imagine you . . . well, you've kept this as a secret, haven't you? No, Leroy, I'm not judging, didn't you hear my story? I had a secret, too. You can trust me on this, I know what you're going through.

No, you don't look gay at all. I just, I tell you, me and my big mouth. I never meant to make you uncomfortable, believe me. But, if I may say, I think it's fate, and not just your mother that brought you here, to me. I know how lonely all this can be. Society has made us feel guilt, shame, and a whole bunch of shit. No, no, please don't go. We don't have to talk about all this if you don't want to. I am serious, we can do it when you feel ready, and only if you feel like it.

Oh, look, Martin is here. Come on, let's help him with the groceries. His managing style is not as relaxed as mine, but together we make a balance. He is so mature for his age.

Hey, Martin, meet Leroy. He's our new guy.

CHAPTER SIX

leroy

LOOK AT ME, FIRST I HATED TAOS AND NOW I'M working on yet another drawing of its mountains. I guess it's like they say: New Mexico is the land of enchantment. I don't think I've ever seen such beautiful sunsets, and the stars, don't get me started on the stars. I keep thinking this is the place where Van Gogh would re-do his *Starry Night*. It's like a black blanket full of diamonds. I never saw this many stars in Dallas.

It's exactly like Samantha told me: "Taos grows into you." I can't believe it's been almost two months since we moved here. So much has happened already, it feels like we've been here for years.

I never expected to actually like this place, but meeting Samantha has been essential to my adapting. To think that I didn't wanna work at the coffee shop, no wait . . . I thought I was gonna hate Samantha. On the first day I met her, I was sure she was a total nutcase. Well, she *is* a nutcase, but the kind of nutcase that you want in your life. The kind you need.

She has become like a second mother to me. Mama is even a bit jealous about her; she doesn't say it, but I know it. I talk about her all the time, maybe I shouldn't. It's just that I feel a connection with her. Samantha dated many men, she married one, she did everything she could to avoid being herself. I did the same. Maybe I still do it. I know I did it to Sharon, I did it to all the other girls I dated or sorta dated before her. I wish I had Samantha's balls to finally just come out. For now, though, I just can't.

The best of the best is that I will be painting my first mural, can you believe it? Samantha told me to choose any wall I wanted at the coffee shop, and she told me to paint whatever I wanted. I was kinda lost. I told Mama about it and she told me it would be nice if I did something related to how I feel about Taos now. I liked that. Mama can be hard sometimes, but when it comes to my art she is always helpful. Her prompt has me thinking, nothing real has come to my mind yet, but I dunno, I can see color dancing in my head. I wanna do a couple of sketches first, you know, to show them to Samantha before I actually start working on it.

Samantha's been really great to me. She's made me read a lot, I've learned more about myself, thanks to her books. She has also offered to lend me some films and documentaries about the LGBT community, but I am a pussy, yes, a pussy, and haven't dared to actually accept them. I don't wanna risk Mama catching me watching two dudes or two girls making out, talking about their wedding plans, or their right for parenthood or whatever.

I would have expected Taos to be as homophobic

as any other small town in this country. But no, it's not like that here. There's actually a friendly gay community. That's what Martin says. He's recently invited me to join him at their meetings and activities. Isn't it funny how life works? My homophobic mother insists that I get a job, and accidentally sets me up at the gayest coffee shop in the Southwest.

Yes, Martin is gay too. But I must say that it took a big argument between us to talk about it.

* * *

Martin and I started on the wrong foot.

It was my second week working at The Spot. I was outside, cleaning the tables on the porch. There was this couple from Colorado out there, Gary and Stephen. They were talking and reading the paper as they did every single day during their stay in Taos. Anyways, I couldn't stop watching them. For me, they were a sight to see.

I know, that sounds weird. What I'm trying to

say is that I liked seeing two men together openly; they seemed so comfortable with each other. I had never seen older men as in love as these two, actually I have never seen any couple as loving and caring as Gary and Stephen. In truth, I hadn't seen many gay couples at all in my life.

So, I was there, cleaning the tables but mostly staring at them when Martin approached me and whispered, "We need to talk."

I followed him. "What is it?" I asked.

Martin was behind the counter, like a boss. He looked at me and said, "What are you doing, man? Have some respect."

"What did I do? What d'you mean?"

"You're staring."

"Staring?"

"Yes, you're staring at them. That's rude."

"I ain't staring."

"You've been doing it since the first day they came here. I've seen you. If you have issues dealing with gay people, then we have a problem."

"No, I don't, we don't . . . I guess I didn't realize I was . . . "

"Judging?"

"What? No, no judging, I swear. It's just, I'm not used to this, they, they're . . . "

"Gay?"

"In love."

"You're telling me you stare at them because they're in love? You expect me to believe that? Listen, Leroy, I'm not stupid, I know how people like you can't understand whatever they find different."

"People like me? Oh, so this is because I'm black."

"What? No, it's not because you're black," he hissed. "You black people think that everything has to do with the color of your skin."

"And it doesn't?"

"No, of course not. It has to do with the fact that you are staring at two gay men, judging them. You're homophobic."

"That's not true! You don't know what you are talkin' about."

We never realized when our conversation became loud. All of a sudden, Lynn pushed the kitchen's door and said, "What the hell is going on here? I can hear you back there! We have customers, you know," she said, pointing to the sitting area.

We turned around, but the only customer was a woman busy with her computer wearing big, badass headphones.

"Anyways," Lynn said, "cut it out. Show some respect."

"That's exactly what I'm telling Leroy," said Martin, but Lynn was already gone.

"Listen," I said. "I wasn't staring at them because I am disgusted with them or anything like that. That's not it at all. And I know this might sound stupid, but they look so nice together, they're a beautiful couple, they seem so in love and so comfortable with each other. You don't see that in Texas all that much, at least not in my neighborhood. That's it and that's all."

Martin looked at me as if I was one of those alien figures from the museum in Roswell. Then he smiled. "They do look nice, don't they?" he said.

"Yes," I said.

"My parents love each other, but they don't have that shine in their eyes when they are together. It's like . . ."

"They've just met and they're flirting," I said. Martin smiled and nodded. He took the towel and continued cleaning the counter. I took that to mean the conversation was over, so I turned around to finish my work.

Before I walked out to the porch, he said, "I'm sorry if I was mean or rude. Was I mean or rude?"

"A little," I said.

"It's just, you never know. You never know when you will find an asshole giving *us* a hard time.

"Us?"

"Us gay people."

"Wait, what?" Had Sam talked to him about me?

"Come on Leroy, you know I'm gay. I know that's why you . . . "

"That's why I what?"

"That's why you ignore me. You're afraid I'm gonna out you. It used to happen to me all the time—before my family and I moved to Taos, that is."

"No, it's nothing like that. One, I didn't know you were gay, and two, well it's not that I ignore you."

"You do. All the time."

I could see where the idea came from. Since the beginning I decided to keep my distance. Why? Because I liked him. He has this magnetic presence, his smile brightens your day, his strong velvety voice. He's skinny and tall. His brown-copper hair a mess, he looks like a trimmed tree with a bunch of brown leaves on the top. He even smells like wood. He smells like a forest.

Martin has beautiful dark skin and these big

glasses that make his eyes look bigger. He has a nerdy look, yes, but a handsome one. I can't stop looking at him.

"I am sorry, it's just, I guess you make me nervous, you being almost like my boss and everything."

"So, you seriously didn't know I was gay?" Martin said.

"No, I didn't."

"Oh, well, now you do. Anyway, I get a little bitchy when it comes to this."

I suddenly felt weak, a cold shudder in my body.

"Leroy? Leroy you okay?"

I sat down on the table across from the counter. He was gay, Martin was gay. How easy, how easy it was for him to say it. I felt sorry for myself. I can't explain it. I can't explain how Martin casually coming out to me made me feel. I started crying.

Martin jumped from the counter and came to me. "Leroy? Leroy what is it?"

Like the pussy I really am, I said, "Nothing." I caught my breath and faked a smile. I was on my way out, to continue cleaning the tables outside, then I went back and said, "Thank you."

"Why?"

"For telling me about you. It takes guts."

"Not really," he said. "Let's hang out one of these days, okay Leroy?"

"Sure," I said, but I couldn't picture myself hanging out with him. Martin, he is so confident, so mature. He has a strong opinion about everything. Politics, environment, art, you name it. He is like an adult in a teenager's body. I don't know, he makes everyone else look like an ass. Even adults.

I like him. I admire him.

Yes, I *really* like him.

martin

Growing up in a conservative town with a very liberal family is an experience within itself; now imagine adding another ingredient: the one child in this very liberal family is gay. The stories I could share! My parents have always been very supportive, but everyone else around them wasn't. My grandparents, my aunts and uncles, my cousins. As a kid, I was constantly bullied.

Until one day I ended up in the hospital. I was molested by an older man at my school. To this day I can't understand why he did that to *me*.

I was in the bathroom. He came in with a trashcan and I thought, *he must be new here.* When I was washing my hands he started talking to me, he asked me how I liked school, he asked me my name. Then he started checking the stalls one by one.

"Oh, is this yours?" he said, and stupid me went to him.

"What?" I asked and then he grabbed me by the shoulders and pulled me inside and covered my mouth. He locked the door and said, "If you yell, I will cut your dick off. So you better do as you're told."

I tried to kick him, I tried to anticipate his moves. But I was too small for him. It wasn't playing cat and mouse, it was playing tiger and mouse. And the tiger hurt the mouse.

Before he left, he said, "And remember, if you say anything about this, I will tell them you're lying, no one will believe you." And before he left he punched me hard. I fell on the floor and he kicked me—once, twice. Two fractured ribs and a broken nose, that's what I got.

My father made it a legal matter. He sued the school, then everybody knew what had happened to me. I was already the weirdo in school. Can you imagine what I became to them after that? My mother decided it was time to leave town. That was no life for any of us.

Protecting me was one of the reasons my parents decided to move. "We've always wanted to experience a more rural way of life," they said. "Yes, outside the system, far from The Man," Dad added. I was too young to understand it then, but I know they did it for me. They did it all for me.

Coming to Taos saved my life in so many ways. I was raised to embrace nature, to embrace diversity, to embrace who I am.

* * *

When I see any slight sign of abuse to kids, I go nuts. When I meet people who show even a slightly homophobic way of thinking, I bark at them as if I were a mother dog defending her puppies.

I thought that was Leroy's case. I thought he was homophobic. He had all the symptoms: he didn't talk to me, and when he did he wouldn't look me in the eyes. Then I caught him staring at that gay couple outside the coffee shop.

And I made such a big deal about it . . . But when he explained with all that sweetness that he was looking at them as being a beautiful thing, the way someone might look at a painting, I felt like shit. So much so that I told him about myself. And I don't tell my secrets to just anyone, not that I'm ashamed of who I am, no. I believe that my being gay is a gift of life, for me and for those around me, so you must be deserving for me to tell you that. My mother says that's presumptuous of me. She's probably right.

Leroy's honesty made me want to be friends with him; it wasn't easy though. I had to ask him a few times before he finally agreed. We went to hear this band from Colorado that was playing at the Garage, which is the closest thing to a live music bar in Taos.

I drove us there. On our way there we didn't talk all that much. It was like neither of us knew what to say, because of course, we had no idea what we had in common. At some point, the episode of him staring at Gary and Stephen came up. What struck me the most were Leroy's words. He said, more or less, "People who stare at gay couples are more curious than hateful." He had a point.

"Why are you curious?" I asked him.

He thought about my question for about a minute, then he said, "Because I have never seen that much love."

We didn't even get to hear the band. We stayed outside, sitting on the sidewalk talking. He told me what it was like to grow up with a single mother who is so damn bossy. I told him about the bullying I went through before Taos. Before long, it was late.

I took Leroy home and, all of a sudden, before he stepped out of my car he said, "I am gay too, you know."

I can't explain what I felt when I heard him say

those words out loud. It surprised me—but at the same time, it didn't.

"But I am not like you," he said.

"Like me?"

"Strong, open. I guess I'm too afraid of who I am. My mother would kill me if she found out."

I didn't know what to say. I don't think I came out with my parents, I think I've always been "out," because they figured it out way before I did. The only thing I could think of to say was, "I understand, and I'm sure it isn't easy, but you can't hide it from yourself, and at some point I'm sure you won't be able to hide it from everyone else."

I guess my years going to counseling and volunteering at LGBT groups have paid off. Leroy smiled.

"Thank you," he said.

I went to bed that night feeling happy. I don't think I came to this world to save gay people from themselves and from others, but sometimes it sure feels that way. And I like it, I like being there for people like Leroy, people who haven't learned to love themselves, to accept themselves.

Ever since Leroy and I opened up to one another, I've been doing nothing but studying him, trying to figure him out. I've seen him with his mother and his sister at some events in the plaza—he certainly plays his "man of the family" character well.

* * *

We are going out this weekend. I told him I would take him cruising, he was like, "Cruising?"

"Yeah, cruising, but forget it, *cruising* has a different meaning here. There are no big studs waiting for young meat, willing to give you head." I nearly laughed out loud.

"Geez, that's pretty graphic," Leroy said, laughing. "So what does *cruising* mean in Taos?"

"It means what it means, getting in a car with a bunch of friends, playing loud music, and driving around town."

"Friends?"

"Yes, my friends from school, you'll like them."

"Are they, you know?"

"What, gay?"

"Yeah."

"One of them is gay, yes, two of them aren't. And don't worry, you don't have to tell them about being gay. And I won't tell either. When you are ready to, you can tell them yourself. They know I'm gay and it's no big deal."

"What if I'm never ready to tell the world I'm gay?"

"Well then you don't, but . . . "

"But?"

"You would be lying. You'd be lying to yourself and to everyone around you. Honestly, Leroy, lying is way harder than just dealing with everyone's reaction to the truth."

"Martin, we've talked about this. I can't, not yet."

"*Yet*, you see, you said it yourself. You won't

talk about it just yet. That means that one day you will."

"I don't know."

Leroy has this sweet face, his dark skin goes perfect with his light brown eyes. Have I mentioned that he has a fantastic smile? Sometimes, when I see him struggling with his own shit, I just wanna hug him, caress his hair and tell him everything will be fine. But I'm sure he would freak out. It turns out he isn't homophobic, he's hug-a-phobic. You know, those kinds of people that can't deal with any type of public displays of affection.

I'm looking forward to cruising tonight. We've been doing it for a year now, my friends and I, since we all got our drivers' licenses. But this time it will be different, I don't know why, but I can feel it already. Tess, Jim, and Luna will like him. And Leroy will like them. We will be a six pack from now on.

School starts next Monday, and for the first time I'm looking forward to it. I can see myself hanging out with Leroy and the rest of my friends. My last high school year. Wow, Leroy is really on my mind. Leroy, Leroy, Leroy.

martin and leroy

"Hey Leroy, how's it going?"

"Oh, I dunno."

"How do you like Taos High so far?"

"Dude, I just had math with this weird, weird, *weird* teacher, I already know I'm going to fail."

"Let me guess. Tall. Skinny. Messy hair. High-pitched voice. Says like ninety words a second?"

"Yup."

"Mr. Fisher."

"Have you had classes with him?"

"Worse than that, he's our neighbor. He's a little too much, but he's a nice guy. His train of thought goes faster than lightning. But don't worry, I have my notes from last year, and I'm great with numbers, I can help you with it."

"Thanks, man."

"How about the people here? Meet anybody that you like?"

"Everyone's cool and friendly. Very different from Dallas. At my old school the new guys always get the cold treatment. Especially the new *gay* guy pretending to be straight."

"Welcome to the Sons and Daughters of Granola-Zen Parents town."

"I see what you're saying. Really, everyone was cool. Look, I got the emails of everyone in my chemistry class. Hey, wanna sit with me?"

"Sure, yeah. Nice choice on the salad over the burger made of *who knows what.*"

"Yeah, you want some?"

"Nah, I'm the nerdy guy who brings his own lunch. The food here sucks."

"I think it sucks in every school in this country."

"It does. And I see your salad does too, it's like a thousand lettuce leaves and the thinnest slice of tomato."

"Yup."

"Here, I have two peanut butter sandwiches, you can take one."

"You sure?"

"Yeah."

"Thank you."

"So, what do you have next?"

"Lemme see . . . Journalism with . . . Miss Wart, is that her last name for reals?"

"Yeah, and she cannot have a better name, she is a wart. A painful wart. But Tess heard she's retiring this year, so she will probably be taking it easy with you all."

"Hey, how come Tess is a junior like me and not a senior like you all?"

"Because she took a year off. Well, her parents did. They went to India on a mission."

"Mission as in Christian mission?"

"Yeah, but without the Christian part."

"What do you mean?"

"See, this is what I've been trying to tell you, we are in the Sons and Daughters of Granola-Zen Parents town. I'm serious, everyone's parents in this town are a little bit crazy-liberal-granola-let's-fight-the-system kinda people."

"Not my mother."

"Who knows, maybe she is a crazy-liberal-granola woman who is in the closet."

"Like me, you mean?"

"Fuck. No, from what you tell me about her I'm pretty sure she'll be out of the closet before you, ha ha."

"That's not funny."

"Oh, sorry, I didn't mean. . . . you're not mad, are you? Leroy, my man. I'm sorry, I didn't mean that, believe me, I was just being. . ."

"An ass."

"A *bit* of an ass. But I'm serious, you don't know what's really on your mother's mind. You don't know what she keeps in the closet. Nobody does."

"What do you mean?"

"Take Tess' parents for example. Before they moved here, they were the most normal couple from Idaho, and now they have harmony and do nature workshops and shit."

"People from Idaho are not normal."

"I guess not, but I'm sure they don't have group meditations on a full moon at two a.m."

"Ha, ha."

"What I'm trying to say, Leroy, is . . . "

"I know, I know what you're trying to say. I know where you're going with this. Maybe I'm wrong about my mother, but you haven't met her."

"We can fix that, take me to your place."

"Oh, no, I wouldn't do that to you, believe me."

"Is it that bad?"

"Yes, well, not with new people. I guess you can say she's nice to everyone but us."

"You and your sister?"

"No, actually she's pretty cool with Amber. I mean me and my brother."

"Your brother? I didn't know you had a brother."

"I do, he's older than me, and well, he stayed in Dallas."

"Is he attending college?"

"No, he's attending jail. He's in jail."

"I'm sorry, man. We don't have to talk about it if you don't want to."

"It's okay. My brother, well he's awesome, you would like him. He's actually the only one who knows about me. You know, that I'm gay."

"Why is he in jail, if you don't mind me asking?"

"Because he's a mess; he's made too many bad decisions. It's pretty much the same old story. Kid starts rebelling against his mother, kid starts hanging out with the wrong kind of people, kid starts stealing stupid shit just to prove he's bad. That sorta thing."

"Wow. You miss him?"

"All the time."

"And, do you keep in touch?"

"I try. When we lived in Dallas, I would visit him every other week, with or without my mom. But now, well, now our whole relationship is based on letters."

"You write to each other?"

"Yeah, I haven't done it all that much lately, though."

"Mmhmm. What about your mother, does she keep in touch with him?"

"That's a good question. I don't know. Maybe she does, maybe she doesn't."

"Your mom sounds like . . . "

"A witch?"

"No, I was gonna say like the character of a Russian novel, but if you prefer witch . . . "

"Ha, ha."

"So, let me ask you this. Are you planning to come out, you know, to her?"

"Nope."

"Not now, or not ever?"

"It's hard, you know, just to think about it gives me the chills. Part of me wants to, but part of me . . . "

"Is afraid."

"Yes. I don't know what she would say or do."

"Tell me more about it."

"No way. You're crazy. I have class now and you do too. Plus, the school's cafeteria is not the most comfortable place to talk. Maybe we can talk about this some other time."

"How about later today. You coming to the coffee shop?"

"I wasn't planning to, I'm only working weekends now."

"Well, you can come as a customer."

"I guess I can."

"It's a date then."

CHAPTER SEVEN
leroy

D EAR KENDELL,
How are you? It has taken me ages to write you, I'm sorry. But I've received every one of your letters.

You should consider going to that writing workshop that you mentioned in one of your letters, you have a talent, man.

That thing you sent me about Gino's story is badass. Does he really have a tattoo for every place he's been to? It sounds like he's had a rough life. Sounds like he's the kind of person you could learn from.

I'm glad he has taken you under his wing, because I'm sure there is a lot of shit happening down there that you are not telling me about.

Things are going well in Taos, actually. Way better than I had expected. I can't wait for you to be free to come join us here.

It's a small town, yes. It has only one Walmart, one Albertson's, three pharmacies, one movie theater, and four coffee shops, but one thing I can tell you, it's got the best Mexican food you can imagine. Seriously.

Remember Sharon? Well, she still texts me almost every day, she didn't take it all too well, my coming here. She didn't even want us to break up. I feel so bad about her, I text her back sometimes, I have even sent her a couple of emails, but I don't think that will help her get over me.

Anyway, school is fine, it's small, as you can imagine, instead of taking classes with 30 other kids in one room, I get to be in classes with more like 20 guys and girls. Only a few of my classmates were actually born here, the rest, just like us, have come from all over the states to build their lives here. I know this is going to sound pretty... well, gay, but this is a healing place.

I have made friends, there is this guy who works with me at the coffee shop, (I'm sure Mama has told you I'm working as a barista), his name is Martin, he's from Oregon, and he's awesome. He's introduced me to his friends, and he's, well, he's just like me. If you know what I mean.

And if you don't know what I mean, let's just say that Mama would not approve of him being my friend. Mama, as you know, pretty well doesn't approve of people like him.

Mama and Amber are doing well. Mama, oh I even dare to say that she is happy. The new school has given her this positive energy. Amber, she is Miss Popularity you know, she got friends right away and now everyone in town knows her. We never have to worry about Amber.

We are good, Kendell.

We are good, but not perfect because you are not here with us. Mama says that she's not sure you'd want to come back to living with us, especially now that we're here in Taos. I refuse to believe that if you had that choice, that you would not be here with us.

This has been a fresh start for us, it can be the same for you, too.

Hope you are starting to make plans for getting out, and I hope they include living back at home with us.

Love, L.

kendell

Leroy, My Man,

Thank you for your letter and for the drawings. The zombie hunters are my favorite, they're fucking amazing. Who could have imagined that you would be able to go from flowers and Greek goddesses to zombies, rifles, blood, and brains?

I am just fucking with you, I know you don't do flowers and Greek goddesses no more.

What are you up to, by the way? Mama did tell me that one of the reasons for her moving y'all to Taos was to get you to work with the artists of the town.

Don't worry if you don't write me as often, I understand. If I write these fucking long letters it's because I miss you, and because being here with nothing to do at night is pretty shitty. We do have our hands full during the day doing chores and shit. But after dinner, everything moves so slow. We get to watch movies two nights a week, so when there's no movie nights I just read and write. I've read so much shit you wouldn't believe it.

I've discovered that writing is pretty badass. I even signed up for that writing workshop they offer here. The teacher is a cool dude. He was in jail once, so he can relate to what we go through, and he knows how to help us get all the pain out, and to keep it out.

I have also started some therapy here. I'm learning about me and about our family, and maybe a little bit about why I did the things I did. I am learning the rough way, though. I can't even explain it.

Now, about Sharon. Stop talking to her. I know you, and I'm sure you feel guilty and everything, but have some fucking mercy, dude. That chick loves you, and she will continue doing so unless you finally do something about it. Just be a dickhead, she'll suffer, yes, but then she'll get over it.

And if she doesn't, well, once I'm out of here I can share some love with her. I always found her pretty hot! Just kidding (kind of).

I'm happy you got that friend of yours, he sounds cool. In case you wonder, yes, Leroy, I understood pretty well what you meant about him being just like you. I even think that someone is having a crush. I respect you and all, but please if something does happen between you two, spare me the details!

What I do wanna tell you, bro, is that you can't keep fooling yourself, you can't keep living a secret. I understand you don't wanna hurt Mama, but listen, if she doesn't understand it, it's her fucking problem, not yours. That is what I've learned from her, if people don't get you, fuck them. Isn't that what she did with her own parents?

On the other hand, I have something big to share, and I don't know how you are going to take it.

I got a letter from Malik. Yes, Malik, your old man.

It seems he heard about me being here and decided to contact me. His were words of support, dude. I'll be honest, I cried like a little girl as I read them. From what I understand he's been through a lot. He obviously asked about you. He told me that if I decided not to write back he would understand, but he also said that if I did decide to write back to please include your address because he wants to contact you.

I don't know how you feel about this. I'm sure you're in shock. I want you to think about it. Malik was always great to me, to us. Until he left, of course. I would like to write him back, but I won't if you don't want me to.

Take your time. Decide what you want, don't talk to Mama about this, though. Don't let her be involved in this. It's up to you, this is all up to you. I'll be here . . . waiting to get the fuck out.

Take care,
K.

leroy

Malik. I stopped thinking about him a long time ago. Father, I don't even know what that word means.

I can't believe he tracked Kendell down. It's kind of a nice gesture, I guess. I wonder what he looks like now. I wonder if I look like him. I wonder what would he think if he knew his only son is gay? Oh, well, that's if I'm still his only son. Maybe he remarried; maybe he's been spreading his seeds all over. Who knows?

Mama never talks about him. Actually, she never talks about any of our fathers. And we all know better than to ask. There are things you just don't ask Mama. Like what happened to our dads? Why did she break up with every one of them?

Malik. I don't know how I feel about him. I'm just glad he reached out to Kendell.

CHAPTER EIGHT
leroy

HEARING FROM KENDELL ALWAYS MAKES ME HAP-py, but at the same time his news shocked me. I told Mama I was going out.

"What about dinner?" she yelled, angry.

"Not hungry," I said.

I went to get my sketchbook and my pastel case; the plan was to walk around, find a spot, and draw my guts out. Mama came into my room first.

"Are you okay?" she asked. I nodded without looking at her.

"It's Kendell, isn't it? He's in trouble again? That's it, right? You better spit it out, Leroy, I'll find out one way or another. I saw you reading his letter, what happened?"

Mama and her monologues. I looked at her, and for a second I wanted to tell her what was up, but instead I said, "Nothing, he's okay, considering where he's at. I just miss him, that's all."

Mama seemed a bit off at first, like she felt bad about thinking the worst, but then she just said, "Fine, just don't be late. It's a week night."

As I was walking out of the house, Amber stopped me. "Can I come along?"

I said no.

She insisted. "Come on, you never ever hang out with me anymore."

Amber was right. Ever since I started working for Samantha and classes started, I haven't paid much attention to my little sister.

"Not this time, Amba girl, but I promise we'll do something this weekend."

"But you work on weekends, Leroy!" she said.

"Well, how about you come with me to work this

weekend, you can be my assistant. I'll even share my tips with you." Amber's eyes brightened up.

"Promise?"

"Promise."

She then opened the door for me, and I walked out.

* * *

I went to the plaza, then walked around downtown. I sat down outside the big abandoned house on Paseo del Pueblo Avenue. I stayed there for an hour or so, but couldn't get anything done. My mind was elsewhere.

I decided to go to what has become my favorite place in Taos: the coffee shop. I thought that maybe talking to Samantha would help—if there's someone you can talk to when things are a mess, it's her.

Martin was at the counter, and the minute I walked in he looked at me and asked, "Hey, you okay? What's wrong?"

"Nothing," I said. He gave me this look that said: "I don't believe you." So I went, "Really, nothing. Hey, where's Samantha?"

"She's out."

"But her car is here," I said.

"She took Clara for a walk. Hey man, I'm serious, you okay? I'm not buying that *nothing* shit."

I couldn't even answer. I felt a knot in my throat. I must have looked as shitty as I felt inside.

He made me some tea and sent me to the storage room; Samantha recently added a small sofa in there so we could rest during our breaks. Anyway, I went straight to the sofa. A few minutes later Martin came in. He got Mike to take his place at the front.

"Leroy, what's wrong, you don't look right. You know you can tell me anything."

I told him about Kendell, I told him about his letter, I told him about Malik, my father. Martin listened to me. He was taking care of me.

I started crying, I couldn't get a hold of myself.

It's like all the tears that Mama forbid me to shed about almost anything stormed out that very minute. Martin held me close, caressed my hair. "It's okay, it's okay," he repeated.

At some point, we were face to face, he was softly wiping my tears, and I went for it, I went for him. I started kissing him. He pulled back for a second, but then he pulled me close to him and kissed me back.

We heard a group of people coming into the coffee shop so we cooled off. Martin stood up and said, "Gotta go work, okay?" I nodded. He smiled and said, "I like you, Leroy. Let's talk about what just happened. Will you wait 'til I finish my shift?" I nodded again. "I didn't bite your tongue out, did I?" he said jokingly.

I felt comfortable saying, "Almost."

I've kissed many guys, guys whose names I never

knew—this was back in Dallas, back in that stupid mall where closeted gays like me looked for action. But none of those men—none of those kisses— made me feel what I feel now.

martin

I started having feelings for Leroy even before we became friends. It's a thing I have, I am either attracted to guys who are dumb as rocks, or to guys who I have nothing, absolutely nothing in common with. Like Leroy.

Oh, yeah, let's not forget feeling attracted to the straightest guys on earth. I think that one is my most common mistake. And I thought Leroy was straight, I mean, it's like he exudes masculinity. Now I can see that, if anything, he is a gay-butch, ha ha.

I have learned my lessons in the roughest way. I've been yelled at, punched, and spit at. I have lost friends. That's why I've been cautious when around Leroy, I didn't wanna jeopardize my friendship with him by taking the first step. Then, I kinda guessed he felt the same about me, but I wasn't sure. *Better to be cautious*, I repeated to myself every time I sensed something from his side. Like that day we were both cleaning the storage and he fell off the stool. We were so close, he smelled like wood, like cherry, like . . . I don't know.

Truth is, I'm still scared shitless about crossing boundaries with him. I know that once our differences were left behind and we became friends, we became close; we became part of each other's lives without noticing it was really happening.

I started picking him up to go to school. He started coming to the coffee shop even though he only worked on weekends. We hung out with my friends, until they also became his friends.

There is one thing that worries me. Leroy is trapped inside, in a closet he keeps building for himself. It goes against what I believe, and let's not forget that it never ends well when you date someone who is not out. But he kissed me. He dared to kiss *me*. It's a big step for him, he's opening a door. That must mean something, right?

Can't wait for these dudes to leave, can't wait for Samantha to come back so I can leave with Leroy. I wanna take him somewhere nice and peaceful so we can talk, or not. A place to just be. I can't imagine how he must be feeling—imagine your father wanting to contact you after so many years of nothing?

Where the hell is Samantha? She and Clara never ever walk at this time of the day, and today, today they had to. Damn it.

leroy

I kissed him. He kissed me back. This is the first time I've done something like this without giving a shit. I came here torn apart and now I only feel butterflies fluttering all over. I just want to kiss him again. I want him to kiss me again. I want us to be together. I want not to care about what anybody thinks.

I wanna have sex with him, it's all I can think about every time I'm around him. Real sex. Loving sex. Not the kind you have in a rush. Not the kind that makes you feel disgusted about yourself. Not the kind you forget a minute later. I wanna have the kind of sex that leaves a smile on your face for the day, the kind of sex that makes your skin hurt from happiness. I want Martin to be mine. I want him.

My first sex encounter kinda sucked, but left me with a strong desire to try again, only I wanted to be with someone I really knew, someone I really liked, someone like Martin.

* * *

"I'm done for the day. Oh, did I wake you? Were you sleeping?" Martin asks me.

I didn't realize I had gone from sitting to lying down on the sofa.

"No, no, I was just resting, thinking and thinking."

"I bet. Too much has happened to you today. Your old man, and me."

"You?"

"Well, yeah. I happened to you today. We kissed. You remember that, don't you?"

I smile. This is what I like about Martin, he says things just as they are. There's no pretend-nothing-happened with him. Ever.

Martin takes his apron off, grabs his jacket, and helps me up from the sofa. We stand close, nose to nose. He caresses my cheek and says, "Look at you with those sad eyes."

As we go out the door Samantha walks in, she looks at both of us and smiles. Hers is a smile of approval, or maybe I'm just imagining things.

"It's a beautiful afternoon," she says. "You guys going somewhere?"

Before I dare to say anything Martin says, "Yeah, we wanna find a spot to see the sunset."

"You guys should drive to the Gorge," Samantha suggests.

"That's a great idea," Martin says, then he turns to me and asks, "You wanna go there?"

I shrug and say, "I don't know what that is."

"Don't tell me you haven't been there."

"I don't think so."

"Well you guys gotta go now," Samantha says. "You afraid of heights, Leroy?" she asks.

"Not really."

Before we leave, Samantha says, "Wait, before I forget. Be careful over there, okay?"

"Careful?" Martin asks.

"Yes, careful."

"I don't understand," I say.

"Well, maybe I'm overreacting, and I'm not suggesting anything here, but I should at least tell you. As I was walking I ran into Linda."

"Linda, our pastry lady?" I ask.

"There's no other Linda in town, Leroy," Martin says.

"Or any other Linda like her in the world, for that matter. Anyway, Linda told me that the other night, a couple was taken into custody, the police found them at the rest area next to the Gorge, you know, *having a good time.*"

"Were they smoking pot?" Martin asks, confused.

"Ha ha, no, well, maybe they were doing that, too, who knows. The thing is the police caught them in the act," Samantha adds. Martin nods and giggles.

"In the act of what?" I ask. "I don't understand."

"Leroy, you are slow sometimes, you know that?"

Martin says. "The couple was probably *doing it* there."

"Yeah, and Linda says the girl's parents made a fuss about it. Well, maybe not that big of a fuss, since I hadn't heard about it 'till now. Anyway, not suggesting you guys are doing anything like that," Samantha smiled, "just telling you guys to be careful."

Martin and I exchanged looks—I blushed, he didn't. Is it *that* obvious that there's something going on between Martin and me?

We say goodbye to Sam. Martin walks by my side as we get to his car, he softly caresses my shoulder before each of us go to our own side of his car. Suddenly I don't feel as confused.

amber

I sometimes daydream. I daydream we are all together: Kendell, Leroy, Mama, and me. I dream Mama has a husband, a wonderful, rich, handsome husband who makes her very happy. In my mind he loves the three of us as if we were his own. He buys us stuff and comes to our school events holding Mama's hand.

I tell her all the time, "You should get a boyfriend Mama, a good, handsome boyfriend."

She laughs and says, "You don't know what you're talking about, Amber, you wait and see how men really are." To Mama, all men are bad. Even her kids! She's nuts. Men are not all that bad. There are some who are good and kind, like Mr. Duval the P.E. teacher. He is really kind and sweet. He's very patient with those of us who can barely bounce a ball. Or Martin, Leroy's friend, he is very nice. He's young, sure, but you can tell he'll grow up to be a perfect gentleman.

I met him the other day; we went to pick up Leroy at the coffee shop. Mama stayed in the car and I went to get Leroy. Martin was there, at the cash register, and he said, "Welcome to The Spot, *Mademoiselle*, what can we get you?"

I said, "I'm looking for my brother, Leroy."

He was so funny, he said, "Oh, a brother? We can certainly have that right out for you. Do you want it with or without whipped cream?"

I like him, that Martin. Ever since he became friends with Leroy, well, Leroy seems happier. He even stopped complaining about us living here in Taos.

I like Taos. I can play outside, I can walk to the store if I want, and everybody is friendly to me. I hope we stay here forever. I hope one day Kendell comes to live with us again. I hope we can all be one big happy family one day.

CHAPTER NINE
leroy

AUTUMN HAS ARRIVED, BUT IT FEELS LIKE SPRING. I am in love. Things with Martin are going great. It's been almost a month since he took me to the Gorge. I've never felt this way before, I don't think I've ever been this close to anyone.

We no longer fear discovery. We no longer keep one eye open when we kiss. We love each other from a distance when we're in public. You know, no touching, no kissing, no smiling too much. Martin is sure our gang can smell it, but no one says anything; not them, not us.

He hasn't once put any pressure on me to come out. Although I know, deep inside, that's what he wants me to do. I know he wants us to be open about our relationship. Or maybe it's just me that longs to stop hiding. For the first time in my life, I feel like coming out. I feel like being honest to everyone. I wanna own it.

I'm just too much of a chicken, like Amber says.

Oh, yeah, Amber knows. After she came with me to the coffee shop a couple of times, she said, "You and Martin, you like each other, yeah?" Just like that. I looked at her funny and a smile crept up on me. She asked the question so plainly, like she was simply asking if I liked rocky road ice cream or something.

"What? Why?"

"Come on, you can tell me. I know about gay love and everything. I watch Glee and Gray's Anatomy and . . ."

I stared at her, completely shocked. It was like the cat ate my tongue.

"I know you're gay, Leroy. Kendell told me a long time ago," she continued, and patted me on the back, like a coach would do. "It's okay, you know? Being gay is super normal."

I was speechless.

"Look, don't worry, I won't say a word to Mama. I can keep secrets. I can keep secrets even without knowing why they have to be secrets. But the truth is, if I know, I bet Mama knows, too."

"Well," I said, "*this* has to be kept a secret because not everyone is as understanding as you and Kendell . . . "

"Oh, these days many people are." Amber added, "That's what they tell us at school."

"Yeah, but then you have people like Mama."

"Mmhmm, yeah, she's not that understanding sometimes."

"Yeah."

"It must be hard, though."

"What?"

"Keeping it a secret. You know, it must be really hard to keep a secret that you love someone. You love him VERY much, yeah?"

Amber is right, it's hard to keep this a secret. And it's weird talking to my baby sister about this secret. And yet, it's not that weird. It's just another step toward me coming out, and it feels good. For now, the only woman I talk to about "stuff" is Samantha. She understands me, way more than Mama. Oh, Mama, one of these days I will need to grow a good pair and talk to her.

I have been drawing a lot lately; I go to the Gorge every time I can. Sometimes I bike, sometimes Martin drops me off and then picks me up. He likes giving me space to work. I sit on one of the picnic tables at the rest area and just work.

My landscapes have improved. I've been playing around with both pastels and charcoal. So I have both, landscapes in black and white and in color. I know it might sound stupid, but even the rocks of the mountain are new worlds for me to discover. I have never felt so comfortable with my work.

Mama is dumbfounded by what I've been doing—in my drawings, of course—she knows nothing about what I've been doing with Martin. She is trying to convince me to put together a portfolio. She says there are a couple of artist apprentice opportunities here in Taos and in Santa Fe during the summers.

I know this would be a great opportunity for me, but next summer will be Martin's last in Taos. He will be off to college. He's applied to a few. He hasn't heard anything yet, but he is so fucking smart. Any school will be lucky to have him.

I can't lie, I'm crushed that he'll be leaving. I tell him that ours is a little bit of a tragic love story. Hiding our love from everyone. He says, "You make it sound like we're Romeo and Romeo." I tell him it sounds corny but it's true, it sucks, we've just found each other and will soon be apart, with him going to college somewhere else and me staying here 'til I figure things out. He says once we know where he's going I should join him. "You shall be mine, Romeo," he says jokingly.

If only.

On the other hand, I got a letter from Malik, also known as my father. I haven't dared to open it. He's been visiting Kendell and Kendell says talking to him has been good. "Let him contact you, it'd be good for you too. Give him your work address to keep Mama out of it," Kendell wrote. He thinks it's best if Mama doesn't know any of this. I bet he's got his reasons, with Mama you never know. Actually, with Mama you always know when something can become a problem.

So I did. I sent Kendell The Spot's address and a few weeks later a letter arrived from Mr. Malik Jones. My father. The man I haven't heard from in years.

I'm afraid to open it. Things are going so well now, I mean, I know I'm still deep inside a closet, hiding who I am and what I feel, but still, what if?

I wonder why he decided to contact us. Why now? What needs to happen in a man's life to disappear for years and then come back just like that?

"I see you still haven't opened that thing," says Samantha as she walks in and sees the envelope resting on the counter.

"No."

"Where's Martin?" she asks a second later. I tell her that I'm covering because he had a meeting with the graduation committee.

"Oh, that's right," she looks for Clara the dog, who's been lying down in her corner since I arrived. "You're getting old and lazy, just like me," she tells her. Samantha stands across the counter, right in front of me, and puts the envelope in my hands before saying, "Don't think about it too much. Just open it. What's the worst that can happen?"

"That he wants to see me."

"And would that be so bad?"

"I dunno."

"Come on, sit with me," Samantha says as she

sits down at a table. I follow her. I take the letter with me.

"Leroy, I'm sure it must have been hard growing up without a father . . . "

"And with a mother like mine," I sigh.

"Hey, hey, hey, we've talked about this before. Your mother, every mother, does everything out of love, and we all make mistakes."

"I know, it's just . . . "

"Things are falling in place now, didn't you just tell me that a few days ago? Martin, your art, it's all happening. The way I see it, in life everything is a circle. That is why we read the tea leaves inside the circle of a cup. That is why the world is round." I must be making a face because Samantha adds, "I know you don't believe in all my crap, but I'm serious. The only way you can close a circle is to start a new one. That starts by reading this letter. Give him, and give yourself, a chance to get over the past."

"If only."

"Jesus, just open the fucking letter, Leroy."

"Whoa, Samantha dropping the f-word? I love it!"

"Sorry. It's just, you young people sometimes drive me crazy. Now, go to the storage room, sit on the sofa, and read. I'll cover you here."

"Well, it is your coffee shop after all."

"Just go."

malik

Dear Son,

It must seem strange that I am writing you. Hell, it must seem strange that I am contacting you and your brother after so many years.

I don't even know where to start.

I fucked up. I fucked up with you two, with Birdie, with everyone that mattered. I'm not sure what you know about me, or what your mother told you guys when I disappeared.

When you finish reading this you will hopefully understand my reasons.

First of all, I want you to know that no day has passed without me thinking of you and Kendell, my boys. Your mother made the right decision by kicking me out of your lives. I was a fuckup, and who knows what could have happened.

Since I was a kid I was a mess, being the son of

alcoholic parents didn't help, but I don't blame them. Ultimately it's up to us to decide which path to take.

Your mother, she tried to change my life. When I met her I was a mess, and she wasn't. She taught me to believe in myself. She bet on me, and did everything she could to straighten me out. And I let her down. I let you all down.

Drugs, alcohol, all those things I left behind when I decided to have a family with Birdie, they came back to me. Or, better said, I went back to them. I lost everything, I lost you three. I lost myself.

Before I knew it I was in jail, doing ten years for my stupidity. I'm not saying all this so you pity me. No. If anything, I'm thankful for these experiences, these difficult growing-up years allowed me to prepare for the future. To prepare for you.

Hearing about Kendell's situation made me realize how much I owe you two. If it's not too late I would like you guys to give me a chance. There is so much I wish to share with you. I'm done with drugs and alcohol. I'm ready to be a part of your lives—a positive part.

Your brother tells me you are an artist. That's a challenging career, one that needs support. I would like to be that support. I would like to see some of your work.

If you feel up to it, we could talk. I am including my phone number and my address here. I would love to come and see you. But, if you don't feel like hearing from me, I will understand and respect that.

Your Father

CHAPTER TEN
leroy

I TEXT MARTIN AND ASK HIM TO PICK ME UP WHEN he's done. He immediately calls me back and asks me if everything is okay. "Yeah, it's just, I finally got the balls to read my father's letter and I feel weird."

I call Mama and tell her that I will be coming back a little later today. "Again?" she asks. I try to tell her that I promised to close The Shop today, but it's useless as she has already hung up. I don't get her, she was the one who made me get this job. Now, because she's jealous of my friendship with Samantha or something, she hates that I work here.

I sit down outside the shop, everybody is gone

now. It's pretty dark. The sun sets earlier in winter. It's a starry night, well, every night is a starry night in Taos. It is something I really love, how bright the nights are here. You can never see this many stars in Dallas.

Dallas. I don't miss it for a second.

Martin arrives. I already feel better. He looks at me and smiles. "You have a sad puppy face," he says, and gives me a quick kiss once I'm in his car. "Where to?" he asks me. I shrug.

"Well I don't know about you, but I'm hungry, I say we go get something to eat and then you tell me all about that letter."

"Sure."

What would I do without Martin?

We have burgers and fries. I let him read Malik's letter; I didn't dare read it to him myself. When he finishes, he puts it back in the envelope and looks at me. "What're you going to do?"

"No clue."

"You don't wanna see him?"

"I dunno. You think I should? He's been gone so many years."

"Well, yeah, but at least he's trying. Plus, it seems he's been there for your brother, right?"

"Yeah."

"Well, if Kendell gave him a chance, and he's not even his father . . . "

"You think I should do the same."

Martin nods.

"We'll see. I don't wanna think about it now, I don't wanna talk about it anymore."

"I understand. Hey, have you . . . ? No, never mind."

"Have I what? Tell me."

"No, forget it, you have enough on your mind now."

"What is it Martin? Tell me, please."

"Have you thought about what we talked about the other day, about talking to your mom? Believe me, I respect your decision. I have no interest in putting more weight on your shoulders."

"I know, I know, I have to talk to her, I just . . . "

"Can't find the courage?" Martin asked.

"Courage? What is that?"

"Don't be like that. You are courageous, Leroy."

"The only brave thing I've ever done is kiss you. "What am I gonna do? My life is a mess."

"Have you talked to Samantha about this?"

"I have, actually, she made me read the letter."

"I mean, have you talked to her about you coming out to your mom?"

"Not really."

"Well, you should. I mean, you know I'm on your side. You know I'm here for whatever you need, but I think Samantha can help you a lot more. Man, you know what she's been through."

* * *

Martin drops me off near my house. We kiss goodbye one, two, three times. Then, things heat up a little. I want him and I know he wants me, but I'm afraid we're both too scared to take the next step.

Martin and I haven't had sex. We haven't even talked about it. Isn't it stupid? I wonder if we're making too big of a deal out of it. I remember Sharon, my one and only girlfriend, was all for it, as if it was nothing.

I finally get out of his car and wave him goodbye.

As I open the door, Mama gives me a card. It's from Sharon. Mama says, "Isn't this the most romantic thing you've ever seen? I mean everybody texts or emails now, but Sharon, sweet Sharon wrote you a card."

I take the envelope from Mama's hands. I feel my face blushing. Sharon. I haven't replied to her texts, her calls, her emails. That's why she's writing, I bet.

"Come on, open it up, what are you waiting for?" Mama says.

"I'll do it later, in privacy, if you don't mind," I say and I walk to my room.

"Oh my God, what's gotten into you?"

I ignore her comment and lock myself in my room.

I lie down on my bed and open Sharon's card. On the front is a photo of that Grumpy Cat, that famous meme that you see all over Facebook and Twitter. The card reads, "It's not me, it's YOU." My throat is already dry and I haven't even started reading what's inside. I've been such an asshole to her.

Well, here goes.

sharon

Leroy,

When u asked me to be your girlfriend I was the happiest woman in the world.

When u told me you were leaving to Taos I felt that world fall apart.

But then u told me, u promised me distance would not matter. And I believed it. Stupid me.

I knew what I was getting myself into, distance definitely is an enemy for any couple, but I thought we would make it work. I thought **U** would make it work.

But then u disappeared.

No texts. No emails. No calls.

My friends ask me about u all the time, I feel so stupid. I tell them that you are doing fine, that you are sad without me, I tell them you text me all the time.

But I am fooling myself. I am sick of lying.

U don't care, I wonder if you ever did. U just got what you wanted and that was it. U used me.

I thought you were different; you made me believe you were different, but all I see now is that you are a fucking asshole like every other guy in school.

I deserve better. So forget about me, cause I have forgotten about you.

Sharon

leroy

Fuck.

Sharon is right. I am an asshole. I used her. Not to have sex, but to hide my own sexuality. I am an asshole. I can't believe I did this to her. I should have broken up with her. I should have come out to her. I should have . . . I dunno, done something but not hurt her.

Lies, lies, lies do this to you. Lies mess up your life. Lies messed up Kendell's life and lies will mess up my life unless I do something about it.

I need to do something about it. It's time I look at myself in the mirror and say, "You are gay." It's time I open up; it's time I talk to Mama. It's time I stop fooling myself and lying about who I am.

But, how? How do I do that? I envy Martin, I envy how strong and brave he is. I envy his honesty. I envy how he owns it. He owns his life, his destiny. Me? I only own my fear.

I can't continue like this. I have to. I have to come out of this closet I locked myself into years ago. My jail. My own jail.

samantha

You want to come out. Wow.

Well, I'm glad you decided to talk about it with me first. I mean, your mother is wonderful in her work, it seems everybody loves her here already. So maybe she'll be easier to talk to about this than you think. I understand where your fear comes from. But I understand where she comes from too, you know?

Being a single mother isn't easy. I am sure that she wants the best for all of you, and in doing so, well, maybe she hasn't always been perfect. None of us are.

Oh, sweetie, don't cry, don't . . . you know what? Cry, cry all you want. Don't repress your feelings, not anymore. That isn't healthy. If you feel this is the time, then it is the time. One has to follow one's gut. Plus, you gotta realize this: You are not alone. You have Martin. You have me, and remember, you have your father. Think about him, I bet it wasn't easy for him to write to you, you know, after all those years of nothing.

Oh, Leroy, my dear. It breaks my heart to see you like this. I understand you, I understand what you're going through. And although I can't promise you that it'll get easier once you decide to come out, it certainly feels better, you know? It feels better to be true to yourself.

Of course I know you and Martin are dating, you think I'm blind? I'm very happy for you two, I can now tell you that I secretly wanted for it to happen. It's just, if you had met any of the guys he dated in the past you would understand. I also thought it would be a good combination. I thought that his being so self-confident, his strong beliefs about LGBT rights, and his sense of community would be helpful for you.

The way I see it, one thing is coming out to people, that is something you can decide to do or not, but coming out to yourself? That is something one can avoid, and it seemed to me that you've been afraid to do this. I see you now and I see a different Leroy, a Leroy who likes himself.

I am serious! Oh, look at you, now you're blushing.

Anyway, I asked you why you want to come out to your mom and you haven't replied. Tell me, is it because you're dating Martin?

It is?

No, no, I'm not saying that's a mistake. It's actually beautiful; it's an act of love. But . . .

How can I say it?

That can't be your reason to take such a big step. See, you'd be doing it *for* someone else, and not for yourself. Coming out is something that one needs to do for oneself. It must be an act of love from you to you. And because I know Martin I know he'd agree with me on this.

Leroy, imagine that you come out to your mom, imagine you tell her about Martin. Who knows how she will take it, but imagine things between you and Martin don't work out, imagine you guys break up.

Not only will you be brokenhearted, but you will regret your decision to come out.

You might even blame Martin for doing it. Who knows, you might even convince yourself that it was all a mistake. Even worse, maybe your mother convinces you that this was all a fantasy and then you'll go back to your confinement, back to the closet. Back to lying about who you really are.

You following me?

Listen, I think it's wonderful you feel strong enough to talk to her, I think it's beautiful that your relationship with Martin has taken you in that direction, but sweetie, you can't, you can't do it *just* for him. You gotta do it because you gotta do it. You gotta do it because you need to be honest about yourself with your own family.

Better? You were hungry, eh? You committed a crime to that muffin, I saw you. Oh, Leroy, it's incredible how I met you just a few months ago and now you are such an important part of my life. Just like Martin and the rest of the people in this place.

This is my family. This is the family I chose. The way I see it, we have our blood-related family, the ones we love because we are attached to them. But I believe the friends we make, the relationships we create also become important, they become family. They become the family *we* choose to have, not the one we were assigned to.

That's why it's been easier for you to talk to Martin and me about yourself. That's why you are talking to me instead of your mother. It's simpler. In a way, you know I will love you and accept you no matter what.

No, I'm not telling you not to talk to her. What I'm telling you is to do it for the right reasons, do it if you are ready to put up with her ideas of homosexuality.

You see, the way I see it, everything in life has consequences. Every little decision we make has its price. You must realize that coming out will bring consequences; now, the question is, are you ready for them?

What do I think? Well, I think you're ready. Just make sure you do it for you and only for you. Take Martin out of the equation. And don't you forget it, Leroy my dear, you have me, whatever happens I'm here for you. If there is someone who knows about the price of being true to yourself it's me, believe me.

Now come on, let's get you some coffee.

CHAPTER ELEVEN
mama

HOW COULD HE DO THIS TO ME? NOW EVERYBODY in town is probably talking about us, as if they weren't talking about us already. Why? Because we are the only black people here. Why? Because I'm a single mother who has a kid from each man in her life. My friends back home used to say that I was too paranoid about people talking about me, but I can't help it. I know how mean people can be. All they want is to hurt you.

And now this!

Being called to pick up my son from the police station is one thing, but finding out that he's been arrested because of public indecency—no, no, no—worse than that, arrested because he was having sex with another boy, oh Lord, that is a very different thing.

I wanna kill him. I wanna kill him. And the kid's parents, how can people be like that? They were all calm and cool about everything. "You must understand," they kept telling me. Understand what? As if *understanding* would solve it all.

I should have left him there, I should have used this to teach him a lesson. Yes, that's what I should have done. Oh, my God, and I thought things were going well. The things Kendell has put me through are nothing compared to this. It's so embarrassing.

He tried to talk to me in the car, he tried to open up and everything, but I told him, "Shut the fuck up, Leroy, you don't get to talk to me, not now." Can you believe him? *Now* he wants to explain. Well, *now* is too late.

Part of me wants to believe that this is him just being confused, a phase. Like when he was a kid.

Like when he used to like dancing in front of the TV wearing my heels. But this, this is a totally new level. A totally new Leroy. He is confused, he must be confused. It can't be true, he can't be gay.

Or is he?

Oh, Lord, what if it's true? What if Leroy is gay? What are we going to do? You cannot change a person from gay to straight. That I know.

This is my fault, this must be all my fault. This is my fault for not giving him a role model. The same with Kendell. He might not be a sissy himself, but look at his life.

No, no, no. This cannot be my fault. I raised them kids as best as I could. I gave them everything I had. Look at Kendell, look how he ended up. And now look at Leroy, being caught giving a blow job in a public place.

This is so shameful.

I can't handle it, no I can't. I don't want more problems, that's why I moved us here. I have always wanted to live a simple life, why can't I?

No matter what I do, things always find a way to turn into shit.

He's got to go. Yes, he's got to go. I don't want him in my house, I don't want him around my Amber. I don't want him in our lives.

That's it. He's out.

And we are too. As soon as the semester is over we are out of here, I ain't staying in this town for everybody to judge me and my family.

leroy

It was stupid, stupid. But it wasn't planned, it just happened.

He had left me at the Gorge where I spent the afternoon drawing. When he picked me up, instead of leaving right away we stayed there, talking. It was cold though, so we got in the car. He even turned the engine on. But then we got to talking, he was caressing my hair, I was leaning on his shoulder, we started kissing.

I noticed he had a hard on, and I couldn't help it. I wanted to touch it, to touch him. He wanted me to do it too.

We were both stupid, it was late already, we should have left. We knew better than that.

But we stayed, we stayed and things started heating up between us. Next thing I know I am pulling his pants off and caressing his thighs, my fingers barely touching his dick. His fingers on my hair, my ears, my back. I was about to go onto it and then we heard the siren. The police were there.

It was so stupid, so stupid of us.

We got caught. We got caught and we were taken to the station. They called home and Mama had to pick me up. Long story short, she is kicking me out. Mama is kicking me out.

"This is shameful! This is embarrassing! I don't wanna see you no more!" she yells.

She goes into my room and throws my stuff out, rips my drawings from the walls. She empties my drawers.

"Take your stuff and leave," she says.

"But where to, Mama, where am I going to go?" I ask her.

She looks at me and says, "Go to your little boyfriend and his fucking family for all I care, I just want you out, now!"

Now Amber comes to my room. She had been sleeping.

"What is it, Mama? What happened?" she asks.

"Go to bed Amber," Mama says.

"But what's going on? Why are you making this mess in Leroy's room?"

"Because he is leaving, Amber. He is leaving for good."

"But why?" Amber cries. "Is this because he's gay?"

Mama looks at Amber and she looks at me. "You involved your sister in your filthy life?" she asks me.

"No, Mama, it's not like that. Mama, I've always known, Kendell knows too. It's okay, Mama. Leroy is gay and there's nothing wrong with it," Amber says innocently.

Mama looks at her, she raises her hand. I run and get in the middle before she does anything she might regret later. Amber hides behind me.

"Just leave, Leroy," Mama says. "Just leave." She turns her back and locks herself in her room.

Amber holds me tight and says, "Don't go Leroy, don't go. Don't leave me alone."

I try to tell her that it's okay, but I don't even believe it myself. "Go to bed, before she comes out again," I tell her, but she refuses. She comes into my room and starts helping me clean it up.

Thank God Samantha came as soon as I called her. I explain to her what happened.

"Do you want me to talk to her?" she asks me. But I know there's no point.

"It'll only make things worse," I say.

Samantha nods, pats my back, and says, "Then, then you're coming with me. Go get your stuff, bring as much as you can."

Amber looks at Samantha and says, "Promise you'll take care of my brother." Samantha smiles at her and answers, "I promise."

When Amber and I finish packing, we say goodbye. I walk her to her room, she is crying, but not once does she say, "Don't go." My sister, my little sister knows I *have* to go. I put her into bed and kiss her forehead.

I knock on Mama's door. "Mama," I tell her, "I'm sorry. I'm sorry you had to find out like this. Mama, Mama I love you," I say.

Not a word. Then I hear movement in her room, she opens the door and hands me a letter, Malik's letter.

"Here, you might need this, I bet he'll be thrilled to see what you turned out to be." Mama slams the door in my face.

So Mama found Malik's letter and she obviously read it.

Samantha and I load my stuff in the trunk of her car. I take a look at my house one last time. Amber waves goodbye from her window.

mama

I don't know how to feel about all this. I am mad, I am fucking mad, but I am not shocked. I've always known about him. How? Oh, the hints were everywhere as he grew up. He was so, so different from Kendell. So feminine. It was pretty obvious that he hated cars, spaceships, and balls. How many times did I have to take my purse out of his hands? He never cared about Kendell not lending him his toys. I remember Leroy with his pretty face dancing to commercials on TV or drawing flowers, butterflies, suns, moons, and stars.

I remember this one time when he took a lipstick out of my purse and drew himself a flower on the cheek. "Don't I look prettyful, Mama?" he asked me. Yes, he looked prettyful, but I could not help slapping him and sending him to wash himself. Because I didn't know better. A gay child is not what you want, not when you are a single mother, not when you are broke, not when you are black.

My son had an *inclination* and there was nothing I could do about it. Yes, that's the word I used to talk about it. *Inclination.* I tried to convince myself that there was always the possibility that it was just a phase. And then he changed, he became Kendell's copycat, so I assured myself it was a phase, just a phase. But now I know it wasn't.

I was fooling myself, pretending that Leroy was just like Kendell, that he was just like any other kid his age. He had a girlfriend and everything, and I was happy. And now this. First Kendell and now Leroy.

I have dealt with situations like this before, with my students and their parents, but it's all so different when it's your family. I shouldn't have kicked him out. Now I risk losing him just like I lost Kendell, but what do I do? He lied, he lied to me, he lied all those years. I can't stand that, what kind of example is that for Amber?

This is my fault, this is all my fault. I should have known better. I should have nudged him in a kinder direction. Things could have turned out so different.

What will he do? I am all he's got.

No, maybe this is where I've been wrong all these years. My kids, my three kids are all *I* got. Oh God, why, why is this happening to *me*?

Was that the door? Did he leave? Did he really leave? What have I done?

amber

I can't believe this is happening. This is not how I pictured it. This is not how I pictured our life in Taos. It's not supposed to be this way. Leroy is not supposed to leave, not him, too. We must all be together, Mama, Kendell, Leroy, and me. It's okay if we don't have a man, a husband to take care of Mama who will also take care of us, but it's not okay that we are torn apart.

It's not okay.

I don't know exactly what happened, I don't know why the police stopped Leroy, but whatever it was I think Mama should forgive him. She must forgive him, or else she will lose him like she lost Kendell. We will both lose him.

I hate Mama, I hate her. She pushes everyone away. We are gonna end up alone and sad. Alone and sad.

I'm gonna tell her. I'm gonna tell her she'd

better do something to bring Leroy back. I'm gonna tell her she'd better get Kendell back, or else I will leave; yes, I will leave, too. I don't care where I go.

I want my family. I want my family back. That's what I'm gonna tell Mama. I'm gonna tell her that she'd better get our family back.

Is someone knocking on the door? Oh, maybe it's Leroy, maybe he's back. Oh, no, it's not Leroy; the one standing behind the door is Martin. Mama is opening the door now. I wonder why he's here. Are those his parents? I hope they've come to convince her to forgive Leroy for whatever he did.

Leroy

I break down and cry in Samantha's car.

"Listen," she says, "you can stay with me as long as you want. Hell, you can live with me forever. Who knows, maybe at some point your mom will change her mind."

"What if she doesn't?" I ask her.

"We'll worry then, Leroy. Don't be afraid. You have me and you have Martin, I bet you even have Martin's parents. Kid, you even have your own father now! You are not alone, don't forget that."

"Do you think she'll come around?"

"Sooner or later she will. Just give her time. Sometimes parents are too stubborn to see how wonderful their kids are no matter who they love or what they do."

"She shunned Kendell, now she has shunned me," I say.

"Then, she is now your past. You have a future ahead. You have just taken a big step, coming out."

"I didn't even get to actually come out. This shit, this shit just happened."

* * *

The night is over in Taos, the streets are open to us; it's like they're embracing us, they're embracing me. The streets of Taos are telling me, "It's okay, everything will be okay, just embrace who you are."

We arrive to Samantha's house. She shows me around and takes me to what will be my room. It is filled with photos of Taos, photos that Samantha took over the years. Seeing these images triggers my imagination.

"I have an idea for the mural," I say. Samantha looks at me, a big question mark in her eyes.

"The mural, your mural. The mural you want me to do at the coffee shop."

"Oh, really? That's great. Tell me about it."

"The title will be: *Embrace Yourself.* You'll like it, I know you will."

Just then, my phone rings. It's Mama.

"Hello?" I say, my voice trembling.